All Eyez On The Crown 2:

Rise of a New Connect

Tina J

Copyright 2017

This novel is a work of fiction. Any resemblances to actual events, real people, living or dead, organizations, establishments or locales are products of the author's imagination. Other names, characters, places, and incidents are used fictionally.

Because of the dynamic nature of the Internet, any web address or links contained in this book may have changed since publication, and may no longer be valid.

More Books by Tina J

A Thin Line Between Me & My Thug 1-2
I Got Luv for My Shawty 1-2
Kharis and Caleb: A Different kind of Love 1-2
Loving You is a Battle 1-3
Violet and the Connect 1-3
You Complete Me
Love Will Lead You Back
This Thing Called Love
Are We in This Together 1-3
Shawty Down to Ride For a Boss 1-3
When a Boss Falls in Love 1-3
Let Me Be The One 1-2
We Got That Forever Love
Ain't No Savage Like The One I got 1-2
A Queen & Hustla 1-2 (collab)
Thirsty for a Bad Boy 1-2
Hasaan and Serena: An Unforgettable Love 1-2
We Both End Up With Scars
Are We in this Together 1-3
Caught up Luvin a beast 1-3
A Street King & his Shawty 1-2
I Fell for the Wrong Bad Boy 1-2 (collab)
Addicted to Loving a Boss 1-3
I need that Gangsta Love 1-2 (collab)
Still Luvin' a Beast 1-2
I Wanna Love You 1-2
When She's Bad, I'm Badder 1-3
All Eyez on the Crown 1-3

I would like to personally thank all my readers and supporters for riding with me in every series I put out. All Eyes On The Crown: Rise Of A New Connect, is based on the kids from 5 of my previous books. I listed the kids and who their parents were below to help out anyone who was confused. I know there's a lot of Jr's in the book and I tried my best to make part 2 easier to read. I know some knew who was who, but there were some who didn't.

Violet and the Connect

MJ, Joy, Alex, Mariana, Andres, Allanah and four more! (I didn't name them all because they won't have a part in the book.)

Ricky and Mateo (Hazel and Ricardo's kids)

The Thug I Chose

Zariah, DJ and James (who Heaven was pregnant with at the end of the series)

Alex Jr. (Ang and Alex son)

4

Polo Jr. (PJ) Tara (Polo and Candy kids)

Armond (Polo and Asia son)

Are We In This Together

Savannah and Mason Jr. (They were the set of twins Zoe and

Mason had in part 1 of the series)

Shawty Down To Ride For A Boss

Aiden Jr. (AJ) and Gabriela (Arizona was pregnant with her at

the end of the series)

Akeem and Brea (Steel and Phoenix kids)

When a Boss Falls in Love

Morgan (Melina and Bruno's first child together)

Loving You Is A Battle

James Jr. (JJ) Patience, Sienna, Cream Jr. (CJ) Who is

Cream's child from a woman named Denise

Darius Jr. (Iesha and Darius son)

The parents may have had more kids but I only named the

children used in this book. I hope you enjoy it!

Previously…

MJ

Today is my twenty first birthday and the day my father handed me the crown. His empire was now my empire and people from all over were coming to witness it. All the late nights, early mornings, the traveling all over the world, long business meetings and instilling the same amount of fear in people is about to pay off. I will no longer be the son in my fathers' shadows but the man running shit. It was a proud moment for my dad and he made sure to let me know this morning when I went by their house.

"Happy Birthday MJ." My mom gave me a hug and handed me keys to a brand new Maserati. I couldn't tell you what it looked like yet, because I didn't see it outside. She probably had it in the garage.

"Thanks ma. What up pops?" He gave me a hug and told me to come in his office.

"MJ, I want you to know how proud I am of you." He pointed to a seat for me to sit.

"You came to me at the age of fourteen asking to be

6

groomed to take over. I thought you were joking and your mom and I had a good laugh over it. Here was my love strung son, who couldn't stop chasing the chick in Jersey, asking to run an empire." I laughed because I tried to get to Morgan every chance possible.

"At fifteen, I could tell you were maturing and that's why I took you on your first mission. You took that mans life along with his family, like it was nothing."

"Once you mentioned the disrespect it was no way around it."

"That's when I knew you were perfect for the job. From that day on, you remained focused and even now with the shit in your personal life, you're still handling business. A man who can block certain shit out to get a job done, is the best man for this job."

"I still love her dad. I swear I'm going back for her when I find Carlotta."

"I know son and she loves you too. Your mom talks to her almost every day. After you take the throne, go to her and put it all out there. You didn't go this long without her, to get

7

her back and lose her again."

"I will." I stood up."

"One more thing son." I turned around.

"You have a lot of motherfuckers on your team now and others who will try to get put on. Choose wisely if you take on new prospects. But always choose a man who has a family that he'll die for. The more a person has to lose, the more loyalty they will show towards you." I nodded my head and gave him a hug.

"Love you son." He patted my back.

"Love you too pops."

I stepped out the office and saw DJ, his girlfriend, Aiden and a bunch of my family coming through the door. This is going to be a family affair for sure. Aiden walked in my direction slow and gave me a half hug. I noticed him staring at Joy who left out but I didn't say anything. The guys spoke to my parents and other siblings before following me out to the barbershop. Afterwards, we were going to the San Juan mall to grab something to wear. I picked my phone up that rang through the Bluetooth.

"Happy Birthday Miguel." I had a huge smile on my face. I know she didn't forget but I sure wasn't expecting a call.

"Thank you Morgan. How are you?" I heard her sniffling.

"I'm good. The baby has me sleeping all the time and I feel fat." I snickered listening to her tell me all about my kid.

"I'm sure you're not fat and even if you gained weight, it's fine because I still love you."

"You do."

"More than I can say. After tonight, I want to take you away and explain why I shut you out and what happened to me. I should've told you sooner but I didn't know how."

"Miguel baby, I would've never judge you for what went down. It must've been really bad for you to treat me like that."

"You have no idea. So can I kidnap you for a few days?"

"Hmmmmm. I don't know if my new man will be happy about that."

"Morgan don't make me fly out there."

"I'm just playing. You can kidnap me if you plan on giving me some of that dope dick I've been missing." I started laughing and pulled in the lot of the mall.

"I miss hearing you laugh baby. I'm going to make it up to you and I'm sorry."

"I miss you too."

"I'm about to go in the mall with the guys. Can I call you before the party?"

"Yes. And Miguel."

"Yea." I put the phone to my ear once the car turned off.

"If by some chance you get too busy to call, please be careful. I know how much protection your family has but with everything going on, you still have to be alert. I would go crazy if anything happened to you."

"I promise to be alert and I'm going to call you before I go. I love you Morgan."

"I love you too Miguel." I hung the phone up and it felt like some of the weight was lifted. I hadn't told her what went down but she was going to give me another chance and it's all I wanted. I had to call my new assistant and have her book a room for us in Turks and Caicos. That's where my parents met and that's where Morgan said was her dream vacation spot. I planned on having our honeymoon there but she could pick somewhere else.

We stayed in the mall for a few hours buying shit for tonight and our ladies. I picked Morgan up a lingerie set a size up from what she's used to be since she pregnant and a pair of Jimmy Choos to rock while I'm making love to her. Yea, red bottoms are nice but my woman didn't care for them like she did these. I grabbed her a new Louis purse and a women's Rolex to match the one she got me. My girl had her own money but I'm not going to have a problem with her spending mine.

****

The clock read eight on my Rolex and it was time to roll out. The party started at nine but my pops wanted all the family to meet at his house for a meeting. I sent a text to JJ and told him not to mention it to CJ. He may have been coming but

I'm not giving him information he doesn't need. Plus Cream and CiCi were all lovey dovey right now and I didn't need him interfering with them. My mom told me they had been trying to get back on track.

"Come here MJ." My mom called out to me. I made my way through everyone and stood in between her and my dad.

"This is the moment we've all been waiting for. Your family and closest friends are here to ride over with you to celebrate and watch you become the most feared man in the world. You are my first born, my heart, my pain in the ass and your fathers' protégé. Tonight you will show the world who you are, with all of us supporting you. I'm so proud of you MJ. I love you." I wiped my moms eyes and hugged her tight.

I hugged my father afterwards and did the same with everyone else. At ten, my dad had everyone get in the SUV's waiting. He said we were all driving over and leaving together. No one is to be left behind.

The truck pulled up to the arena and it was beyond packed. Valet opened the doors to all of the trucks and we stepped out and waited for everyone to get together. Security

12

was standing outside our trucks like we were the first family; well I guess you could look at it like that. I pulled my phone out as we waited and called Morgan.

"I thought you forgot." She said when she answered.

"Never baby."

"Have fun and enjoy yourself. Please call me when you get home. I won't be able to sleep until I know you're ok."

"I will." We said goodbye and my dad had us all go in. There was a VIP section taking up half the space. It was enough room for all of us but my dad had a spot in a different area for me. He had me sit in there and wait. I could see down in the crowd from the window. The door opened and I couldn't do anything but smile.

"I should've known you'd be here. My mom kept bringing you up."

"Why didn't you send for me?"

"I didn't think you would come. Damn I missed you." She backed up and locked the door. I shut the curtain to the window overlooking the crowd and moved towards her.

"What are you thinking about Miguel?"

"How I'm about to make love to you?" I unzipped the back of her dress and saw she wore no panties or bra. I kissed her collarbone and her head fell back. She moved my hands to cover her breasts as she turned her face to kiss me. I bent her over forward and my hand was on the back of her neck, sliding down her spine and to her ass. I got in a squatting position, spread her ass cheeks and stuck my face inside. Her right leg shook uncontrollably as her juices seeped out.

I stuck one finger in her ass, another in her pussy and she almost fell. After giving me more to drink, I pulled her up and stared at her. Both of my hands were on the side of her face. I leaned in to kiss her and felt her tiny hands on my buckle. I kicked my shoes off when she got my jeans and boxers down and lifted her up. She bit down on my neck and shuttered when I entered her. I loved the way her pussy curved to my dick.

"You good Morgan."

"Yessssss. Oh God yessssss." I had her moaning in my ear as I hit every spot she had.

"Baby. I'm sorry but I'm about to cum." She nodded her

14

head and slipped her tongue in. We both stifled our moans in each other's mouth when we came together. I fell on the couch still inside her. A few minutes later we were back at it again.

"I'm glad you came." I was still trying to catch my breath after we finished. We were up here for a long time and didn't care if anyone was looking for us.

"I wouldn't miss your birthday baby." There was a knock at the door.

"Stay right here." I moved her on the couch, threw my clothes on and cracked the door.

"Hey MJ. Your dad told me to come get you." My assistant said and tried to push the door open.

"Yo. My girl in here. What you doing?"

"Oh I'm sorry. I thought you were alone."

"Even if I were. Don't take it upon yourself to invade my space. Tell my father I'll be down there shortly." She nodded her head.

"Yo." She turned to look at me.

"Did you do what I asked earlier?" This bitch had the nerve to suck her teeth.

"Yea." I glanced back at Morgan and saw she was fully dressed and opened the door. I didn't have to say another word because the look in my girls face let me know she was about to handle it.

"What's your name sweetie?"

"Elaina. And my name isn't sweetie."

"Hmph." Morgan got in her face.

"I know how fine my man is but if that's a problem, you need to hand in your resignation letter. He hired you as his assistant as a favor to your father but don't get it twisted." Elaina looked shocked.

"Oh yea. He tells me a lot. Now, as I was saying. He has one time to tell me you hit on him and I'm going to make sure you come up missing." I grabbed Morgan by the waist and kissed her neck. My future wife is a beast.

"I apologize and it won't happen. MJ, I handled that for you. Enjoy the rest of your night." Morgan moved my hands and went back in the room. I heard the water running in the bathroom and found her washing up. She grabbed me by the jeans, took them down and washed my dick off.

"Fire her."

"Morgan." She looked at me.

"If you don't, I walk."

"You'll leave me over my assistant."

"No. I'd leave you over a woman whose plotting to get at you. That chick has lust and love in her eyes for you and before you say it, yes I do know. She tried to get in here when you had the door cracked, she had an attitude the second she saw me and was ready to disrespect me, until I got in her ass. Elaina is a problem and if you plan on keeping her around, then I know it's a problem you want." I sat Morgan down and lifted her chin to look at me.

"Morgan, you're all the woman I see and that's never going to change. I understand she made you uncomfortable but she is a good assistant. Does she have a crush on me? Probably, but so do a lot of other women. If I fire every woman for a crush, I'll never have an assistant."

"Trust me MJ. It's not going to end well with her."

"Do you trust me?" I asked and she said yes.

"Then trust I will handle her if she gets beside herself."

17

"Fine MJ." She hopped up and went to the door.

"I'll see you later."

"Morgan."

"Go take the stage to get your crown MJ. You deserve it." She slammed the door and walked out. I ran my hand down my head and stepped in the hallway to see my assistant standing there typing on her phone.

"Trouble in paradise." She said without looking up. I put my mouth to her ear to make sure she heard me.

"Elaina, remain professional and you have a job. If you get out of line, not only will you be out of a job but you'll lose your life in the process." Her mouth hit the ground as she stood their stuck on stupid.

I walked downstairs and went to the stage. I stood there waiting for my dad to introduce me. When he did, I stepped up and received applauds from the crowd. I looked around for Morgan but I didn't see her.

"Thank you." I said into the microphone and waited for them to get quiet. The introduction was more or less for them to know who I was and that my father is no longer the go to man. I hugged him and took the microphone.

"This is a moment I'm sure everyone knows I couldn't wait for. My pops is a legend as we know and ran his empire with an iron fist. All of you know how he handled things and nothing has changed. I'm just as ruthless if not worse and with a lethal team behind me." I nodded to all my family over in VIP.

"I'm the man you never want to piss off." I stared at Elaina who looked scared as hell.

"I'm the man who will take no shorts if you try and fuck me over." I surveyed the crowd and everyone had their eyes glued on me.

"Last but not least. I'm the nightmare that won't go away." I looked out at all the kingpins, dealers, leaders of cartels, and a lot of other important people staring at me and waiting for me to finish but something was off. I knew it, I felt it. My pops told me never to ignore the feeling. I observed some movement in the crowd. I saw people in uniforms spread out along the walls looking directly at me.

I glanced at my dad and with my eyes, told him to get

my mom off the stage. I did the same to where my family was and slowly they were all moving out.

"Fuck you MJ. I'm taking everything you got." I heard in the audience. I couldn't tell the voice because everyone turned around and began asking who the fuck he was.

"Let me see you take it." I hopped off the stage and the crowd parted down the middle for me to get this nigga. I wanted to know who thought they would come here and try to attempt to take my spot. I began to walk but stopped when I heard her.

"Miguel." I turned around and Morgan stood there with something strapped around her.

"WHAT THE FUCK?" I ran to her and she put her hand up and told me not to touch her. There was only a minute left on the timer.

"MJ, I went to the bathroom and they were dressed like the staff. Baby, I didn't know. It was so many of them." She was hysterical crying and I was fuming. I could see people wondering what was going on. I pressed a number on my phone and waited for the person to answer. I wiped Morgan's eyes and held her hand tight.

"DO IT NOW!" I yelled into the phone and all the

lights went off.

Once the lights went off, any electronic devices people had, ceased to function. You couldn't use the lights from any cellphones nor could it be used at all. I pulled my hi tech night vision glasses out my pocket, put them on to see in the club and saw people running everywhere. I noticed the people in uniforms began to disburse but were running into shit, the same as everyone else. We planned for some bullshit to happen but not the part with someone strapping a fucking bomb to my girl.

I turned back around to Morgan who had been squeezing my hand tightly. I noticed the timer on the explosive went blank, which gave me time to remove it. I took the straps off her shoulder and let hit fall to the floor. I grabbed her hand and ran out the back door, where I found all of my family.

"Are you ok?" I checked over Morgan's body and she hugged me tight.

"I'm ok baby." I wiped her eyes and placed in her in the truck.

"Meet me at the spot." I told all the guys.

"Turn them back on." I said in the phone once my dad said all of my family were accounted for.

My pops was yelling for everyone to get in the car. As we pulled off and were halfway down the street you heard an explosion. The ground shook and the windows on the truck rattled. I felt sorry for whoever didn't make it out because not everyone deserved to die. Unfortunately, no one lives forever.

"Stop crying Morgan and tell me what happened." I ran my fingers through her hair as she laid on my lap.

"After I left you, I shoulder checked your assistant because she was still outside. I know you told her to leave. Why was the bitch still standing there?" She stared at me and I didn't say anything. Elaina was out there when I walked out the room but it made me no never mind. Now that she mentioned it, I'm going to find out why she didn't bounce.

"I went downstairs and saw a few guys standing there staring at me. I didn't pay it worry because we were supposed to be safe. I could hear your dad introducing you and people were running in the direction of the room to hear you speak.

23

They love you baby." She smiled and ran her hand down my face.

"Someone grabbed me as I began walking to where the family was and led me to the back. Some dark skin dude barked out orders and said he wanted your head and I was the bait." She sat up and looked at me.

"MJ, I'm not going to ask questions because this is the life you chose and my father always said, *"Living the life with a man that's going to have so much power will bring enemies from every where. Most of them won't like him just because of the power and others won't for their own reasons and until they're known, always watch your back."* Do I need to watch my back MJ? Are you going to keep me safe or should I go into hiding? I can't have your back with the baby?"

"Morgan, I would never ask you to have my back but I love you for wanting to. I promise to keep you safe and as far as watching your back, that's what I'm here for."

"But I don't want anything to happen to you."

"I trust my team Morgan. We've been rocking for years and they know what will occur if they even thought about

24

crossing me. You will be protected as if you were my mother."
I used my mom as an analogy because my pops made sure she was safe at all times. He didn't care if something happened to him as long as my mom was good, he was.

"Ok." She seemed to be ok but I can tell she's still skeptic about it.

I had the driver take her to my parents' house. I got in my own vehicle and drove to the spot separate. I needed this time to think. Who the hell was coming for my spot? Whoever it was had this shit planned out perfect, which told me there is definitely a rat in our camp. The question is, who?

I took a different route to make sure no one was following me. However, I did notice a car at the far end of the block from where the spot was. I zoomed by it to make it seem as if I didn't know they were watching and made a call.

"Yo. You got DJ with you?" I asked James Jr. The two of them left out ahead of everyone else.

"Yea what's up?"

"Where AJ?" I sat in my car monitoring the situation.

"Right here. You good cuz. What's going on?"

"I need you and DJ to get in your car and drive down the street. You'll see a car parked on the left hand side. Speed past it but wait down the road for my call."

"What you want with AJ?"

"Tell AJ and Alex to come out exactly two minutes after you and do the same thing. However, when they pull out the spot, I'm going to call you and I want the two of you to walk up behind the car as they ram their vehicle in the side of it. Pull those motherfuckers out and bring them to me."

"No doubt." James Jr. hung up and a few seconds later I saw them do exactly what I said. I called AJ and they did the same. I got out my car and went inside to find my team there but one person was missing.

"Where is that mother fucker?" Darius Jr. yelled out. I walked in and heard him saying CJ was the one who called me out at my crowning. He made it clear that my spot is where he wanted to be. I guess the gun trafficking world was beneath him, so he's reaching higher up. I never saw CJ because I had run back to check on Morgan.

"Not sure, but he is the least of my worries. I want to

know who the fuck thought it was ok to come in and try to attack? CJ may want my spot, but there's no way in hell, he was alone." I say try because the lights went out before anything could occur.

A few minutes later, my cousins came in with three guys dressed in black. I took my gun out my waist and walked up on them.

Phew! Phew! I shot the first two in the head. I only needed one alive to answer my questions.

"Who are you?" I got down to eye level in front of him.

"Fuck you puta." I chuckled at his ignorance. For one...he wasn't Spanish and he sounded dumb as hell trying to speak the language. And two... they always talk shit when they get caught.

"Wrong answer bro." I shot him in the kneecap, brought over a chair, sat down in it and lifted his face with the tip of my gun.

"I'm going to ask you again. Who sent you?" He remained quiet. I shot him in the other kneecap and asked my brother to bring Nigel out.

27

"Ahhh shit man. I'll talk." He screamed when he saw Nigel.

You see Nigel was a fifteen foot African rock python. He was quite a beauty to be honest. He was yellow and brown with a triangular type head. He was about twenty feet long and weighed a little over a hundred pounds. I picked him up on one of my trips to South Africa a year ago and had him ever since. He's only killed twenty people and today would be twenty-one.

When my sister said she heard I was a beast, every story was true. My father may have done some foul shit during his reign, but the shit I've done, is far worse and even he can't believe it. My mom always told me, she doesn't know where my mind goes when I have to erase people from the earth but she's glad, she'll never be one of them. I nodded my head to Alex and he opened the crate. Nigel began to slither his way out.

"The only way to keep Nigel from you, is to tell me who sent you."

"Please man. I got a family."

"You think I give a fuck about your family? Matter of

fact, AJ get his info out his wallet and send two of your best guys there to kill them." He begged for his family's life but I ignored him.

"This is my last time asking you." Nigel was now by his foot and he couldn't move because well, his kneecaps were gone. He started moving up his leg.

"Ok man. It was this guy named Armond but he's working for some chick. I don't know who she is but they're planning a take over. Oh shit man. Can you get him off me?" Nigel started to wrap around his body.

"Why? What's the reason?"

"They're seeking revenge for their parents. They want you, your family and anyone else close to you. There's also someone in Jersey working with them."

"Who?"

"I don't know. Tonight was our first job." I stood up and went to leave.

"YO, CAN YOU GET THIS THING?"

"Nah. You deserve what's about to happen. Be lucky it's almost over." I said as I watched Nigel wrap his last body part around him.

"Hold up MJ. I want to see this shit." DJ yelled out. I began walking out the room and could hear all of them yelling, *"Oh shit."* I swear they were amateurs but that's my family. I poured me a shot of Remy and waited for them to finish with their fascination. I could hear DJ cursing somebody out for trying to sick Nigel on him.

"Yo. I'm fucking your brother up. Aunt Violet just going to be mad. He plays too damn much."

"What he do?" I sat back in my chair at the head of the table, twirling my gun in my hand.

"Tried to sick the damn snake on me. What if that motherfucker really got me?" I shook my head because Alex did that to anyone he thought was afraid. Everyone came in the room and sat down.

"I'm fucking you up Alex."

"Whatever, scary ass." I sat my glass on the table and stood up.

Everyone had their attention on me. I glanced at my phone that went off and saw it was a message from Morgan. I opened it up to make sure she was good. I had to close it right back. She had no clothes on and sent a pussy shot. I continued the meeting like it didn't make me want to run home, however, business had to be handled first.

"Morgan told me it was a lot of them but the one barking orders had dreads. They were dressed as staff too, so from here on out trust no one. We all have maids, nannies, drivers and some of us have too many women coming and going." I glanced over at Darius and he smirked. My cousin was a damn male ho and we all knew it.

"We may have had these people in our lives for a while but they may have switched sides for reasons unknown. Everyone is a suspect as of right now. Tomorrow we're going to have some fun with the owner of the club and his family. The way I see it, is the only way they could've gotten the uniforms, employee badges and other shit, is if someone helped from the inside. They knew how important this event was and still allowed someone to come in and attack." They all nodded their head, agreeing with me.

"People know exactly who we are, therefore, should've

come to us. Now I have no choice but to take away their family." No one said a word. I'm not taking any shorts and they will learn, I am my fathers' son.

We all talked for another half hour when I gave specific instructions on what to do if anyone came across CJ. We had to keep James Jr. calm because he was so mad; he wanted to search all night for him. I told him that he will need his father soon enough and to be patient. I locked up and drove home thinking of how CJ did this.

The dread head dude may have barked out orders and was following some chicks' orders, but CJ knew exactly where we would be. His ass was going to wish he never crossed me. Cousin or not, his ass is good as dead.

"I love the photo you sent me." I whispered in Morgan's ear when I got out the shower. I dropped her off at my parents but she knew I was coming home and wanted to be here. I wasn't worried about her leaving my parents house because the estate is like the presidents house. Security is everywhere, no one on the outside could see in and the gates are too high for anyone to try and climb.

"You did huh? I think you need to handle that." She tossed the covers back to expose her birthday suit and I damn sure took advantage of her body all night.

Joy

I see people are really trying to kill my family. It was the day after MJ's party and we were summoned to my parents' house this morning. My mom was putting the food on the table and Morgan was sitting on MJ's lap in the living room. I swear they get on my nerves with their lovesick ass. I'm happy they're together though. He has loved her forever and the feelings are mutual. I guess absence does make the heart grow stronger because you would assume they've never lost contact.

My dad came in the room looking energized as hell and smacked my mom on the ass. I sucked my teeth and went to answer the door. It was DJ, Darius and the rest of the guys in our family. I shut the door and heard a small tap. I opened it up and there stood AJ looking sexy as hell. I tried to leave but couldn't get away fast enough.

"Come here Joy." He grabbed my hand and pulled me out the door. I noticed he didn't move as fast but then again he recently woke up. I admired him for still having my families back.

"What?" I stared at him.

"I'm sorry about the shit Shayla told you. Yes, I used to deal with her but I told you after the first two weeks we spoke, I broke it off."

"Yea ok."

"I don't have a reason to lie. You of all people should know, I keep it a hundred regardless of how it may hurt." I didn't say anything.

"Joy, I wanted to make us official the day I came but the bullshit happened."

"Why would she make it up AJ?"

"Joy she wants your spot. We've gotten very close and a nigga is falling in love with you." I smirked and put my head down to kick the rocks.

"Look at me." He lifted my head.

"Tell me you don't have any feelings for me and I'll leave you alone." He leaned in and I should've moved away but I didn't.

"I want you AJ but-" he placed his lips on mine and

pulled me closer to him.

"I could kiss you all day." I told him and kept my arms wrapped around his neck.

"Then why you stop?" Someone cleared their throat and it was DJ.

"It was nice knowing you man. Once uncle Miguel finds out you trying to bone his favorite daughter. He's going to kill you."

"DJ. I'm not his favorite." I said walking in the house.

"Bullshit. Yo! Who is uncle Miguel's favorite child?"

"JOY!" Everybody in the house yelled out and I went to my dad.

"It's ok Joy. We know you're his favorite but he stills gives us everything too." My sister Allanah said making everyone laugh.

"You are my favorite Joy." He whispered and kissed my cheek.

I sat down at the table and AJ sat next to me. My mom had a grin on her face while MJ and my dad paid us no mind. Alex, however, notices everything and had a sneaky ass grin on his face. I wish he would go back to speaking to Gabby because then he wouldn't be in my business.

"Pops, don't you think Joy should be sitting closer to you? I mean, why is her and AJ so close?" He shoved some rice in his mouth. My dad looked at me and AJ.

"Alex, where did you expect him to sit? There's no room anywhere else."

"I'm just saying pops."

"Alex, cut it out." My mom said giving him a threatening stare. He sucked his teeth. I mouthed the words, *"Thank you"* to her. She knew as well as I did, what Alex was trying to do.

Ever since him and Gabby stopped speaking, he's been making everyone around him miserable. Shit, it's his fault they're not speaking. I knew from all the talks Alex and I had, he wanted to settle down. He never had a contender for that spot until he went to Jersey.

My pops and brother had him running up in mad chicks. He kept Julia as his girlfriend to keep her stupid ass from committing suicide. We kept telling him to let her kill herself, but he felt bad.

"I called all of you over here because what went down at my party can never happen again at any event we throw." MJ said standing up. I saw Morgan staring at him with love in her eyes. That's what I wanted with AJ and hopefully one day we'll have it.

"How do you think they knew what was going on?" James Jr. asked.

"CJ." I heard everyone suck their teeth. My cousin Cream had the most disgusted look on his face. CiCi put her head down. I know she felt bad because she helped raise him and here he is, turning against his family, for power.

"CJ is working with some heavy hitters from another country. I can't say for sure from where, but I'm thinking, these are the ones who have or had beef with our fathers."

"I say we get his ass and kill him." James Jr. looked at his father who walked out the room. It had to be hard listening to them speak of taking one of his kids' lives, even if it came from his other son. I stood up and walked out on the porch where he was. Cream and I had a good relationship and when

38

my dad would make me angry, I would call him and he'd calm me down. I sat down next to him and rested my head on his shoulder.

"How you been Joy?"

"I'm good. How are you?"

"Honestly, I don't know. My son is causing major problems within the family and business. As a parent, I don't want him killed but when it comes to loyalty, he has none. I can't stop James Jr. or MJ from getting him and I'm not sure I want to." I stared at him.

"What if you talk to him? Do you think he'll stop?" I asked trying to find a way to get CJ out of hot water with the family.

"I have Joy; hundreds of times. He thinks he knows everything and the world owes him. I took him from his mom because she not only kept him from me, but abused him as well. At first, he was ok with the living arrangements, but as the years went by he started changing. The way he treated my wife as if she did something wrong, didn't sit right with me. He disrespected her on a few occasions and I almost killed him, myself over it." My mouth hit the floor.

"I love all my kids Joy but when you disrespect the woman who raised you and gave you everything you ever wanted, that's where I step in. CiCi is the nicest person in the world and everyone knows that. It's been plenty of nights she cried to me, trying to figure out what she did wrong to make him treat her that way. I hated seeing her cry and it tore me up on the inside." I was shocked because CiCi is just as he described. She has never raised her voice to her kids but they knew when she gave them a look, to cut it out. They loved their mom to death and I'm sure it's hurting all of them to find out CJ has a part in attempting to take my brother down.

"What are you going to do?"

"Nothing. MJ has to do what he needs to and I'm behind him all the way."

"Hey Joy. Are you ok baby?" CiCi said sitting on the other side of him.

"I am now." She smiled and he kissed her lips.

"Joy can you give us a minute?" CiCi asked and I stood up.

"Yup. I love you two." I kissed both of them on the cheek.

"James, I love you and I'm ready to give us a try again." I heard her say as I closed the door. My dad told me, Cream's ex, who is CJ's mom had been causing a lot of problems in their marriage and I guess it's taken a toll on them. Since they've been here, it seemed as if they were getting it together.

"Where you been?" I heard and was pulled away into the downstairs bathroom.

"Are you crazy? If my father.-" AJ shushed me with his lips and lifted me up. I had my arms around his neck as he placed me on the sink and unbuttoned my jeans. I lifted up to help him get them down, along with my panties.

"Sssssss AJ. Shit baby." I moaned out as quiet as I could. His tongue snaked in and out my pussy as he went to work on it.

"Damn you taste good baby."

"AJ, I can't hold it in. Oh my gawdddddd." I let my cream shoot in his mouth. My body was shaking as he continued. I put my arm in front of my mouth and bit down hard as another one ripped through my body. I heard him fumbling with his jeans. There was no way we could have sex. I was a virgin and could guarantee I'd be making a lot more noise that this.

"We can't AJ." I hopped off the sink and grabbed a rag to clean up. I handed him some mouthwash and a rag to clean his face.

"You're right." He lifted my face to his.

"When I get you, I need more space than this." He smacked me on the ass and let me walk out the bathroom first.

"Ugh ahh bitch. Let me find out AJ was in there breaking down them virgin walls." Ricky said laughing and I had to shush him. He wasn't loud but I hadn't told AJ, I've never been penetrated.

"No. He only ate my pussy."

"Girl why didn't you let him do it at your house?"

"You know he can't come over unless DJ does."

"Bitch bye. You better get DJ drunk at your house and handle your business. Let's go. Uncle Miguel looking for you."

He grabbed my arm and we went in the dining room where everyone was.

"Where's AJ?" Alex said smirking. I shrugged my shoulders and Ricky threw a spoon at him.

I loved my family but Alex was pissing me off. AJ walked in a few minutes later and no one paid any attention. The rest of the night we text each other as we sat in the same room. I hoped and prayed my dad didn't look at the tapes. He had cameras all through the house and if he watched them, he'd know where I was and could probably guess what I was doing.

I let my head rest on the seat and put my feet up on the one across from me and closed my eyes. I was on the jet back to the states to retrieve all my things. I didn't need anything because it could all be replaced but I wanted to check up on this PJ dude.

After he said that shit to me the last time I saw him, I wanted to know more then what was on the database, I had access too. Because of my pops, we were able to retrieve a lot pertaining to people's background and everyday life. If I really wanted, I could have his phone tapped and surveillance put on his house and he won't even noticed.

Something about the way he knew the attacks were coming let me know he has a part in it. I wonder if he knows who tried to attack at Miguel's crowning or part of it. I also need to find out who his father is. Maybe that will give me some insight of who he is. His pops never signed his birth certificate so it was harder to find out where he came from. He had to be a fuck nigga too if PJ was.

44

I told the pilot I'd be back shortly and jumped in the car with AJ. I asked him to pick me up because now that we're targets, using a driver from any company is out of the question. Plus it's the only reason MJ let me fly alone over here. He may be my brother but when he says certain things, I don't give him a hard time.

He has all of our best interest at heart and I honestly believe him and my parents would kill everyone if something happened to any of us. Shit, MJ had to talk my pops into stepping back when the accident happened to Joy.

"What up?" I slapped hands with him when I sat down.

"Nothing. Just here to get my things and be out."

"Alright." He started the car.

"Look, I need you and my sister to talk." I blew my breath out and stared out the window.

"Alex, you and Gabby don't have to speak all the time but you do need to have a conversation about my niece or nephew."

"She said it wasn't mine." He gave me a crazy look.

"I cursed her out over saying that stupid shit. Gabby

may be a pain in the ass, spoiled and have a nasty attitude when she wants, but being a ho, is far from who she is."

"I don't know AJ. We both said some foul things to the other."

"Listen, you two don't ever have to speak again. If I had a woman claiming she was pregnant by me, I'd at least be cordial for the baby. I know you didn't make the decision with her to keep it, but it's nothing we can do now."

"I hear ya. I'll speak to her about it later. Let me get my things out of here first."

He nodded his head and we drove to the house. It was two cars sitting in front with tinted windows so we drove down the street to monitor who got in and out.

Mateo got out the car and walked to pretend he was a passerby. When he walked past it he sent me a text and said to come back. AJ parked, we got out and sure enough it was Brea, Zariah and Gabby in one car and DJ, James Jr. and Darius in another one.

"What the fuck y'all doing here and whose cars are these?" AJ looked as confused as me.

"I know you didn't think we'd let you come here alone." DJ said and told us they were rentals.

"AJ got me."

"Yea, well that's two of y'all to a bunch of ghosts; since we don't now who's after us." He said that because we had no idea who's behind the shit going on.

"Hurry your ass up because my mom cooked and I'm hungry." James Jr. said talking shit. I noticed Gabby didn't get out the car and decided to walk over and speak. I handed Zariah the keys and she smacked the back of my head and told me not to yell at her.

"Get out Gabby." She rolled her eyes and sat there pouting.

"If I ask you again, I'm going to help you out." Silence. I opened the door, lifted her up and stood her next to the car with me standing in between her legs.

"Whose baby is it?" She kept her head turned looking down the street.

"Gabby."

"Yours Alex ok. I was mad you hadn't contacted me

since I blurted it out at the college. I'm not looking for you to help me so don't worry about shit over here. Handle your other baby mama in Puerto Rico." I laughed at her being mad over Julia. I made her face me and she wiped the lone tear from her eye.

"There is no other baby Gabby. I was mad at you too. I know we're young and should've known better but I want this baby." I rubbed her stomach and she moved my hand.

"Stop being a brat. You know you want me here." I put my hand on her small pouch and smiled. I wasn't ready to be a father but what could I do now? I would never ask her to get an abortion.

"Believe it or not, I was fine without you."

"Yea ok. Come on." I held her hand in mine. She didn't put up a fight and followed me.

"Alex."

"Yea."

"Is she really pregnant by you?" I stopped.

"No. I just told you, I was mad at you too. I don't even know how I slipped up and got you pregnant."

48

"This pussy was too good to pull out, that's why." I started laughing.

"Nah. You had a nigga hypnotized by the way you sexed me. I never had a woman do me that good."

"Woman."

"Gabby, you and Julia are the youngest females I've ever slept with." It was the truth though.

My brother and I had access to many women from every ethnicity and they had no problem sexing us. I think it's the reason we are both ready to settle down at such a young age. We've had our share of threesomes, orgys, switching up and all the other freaky shit we could do. It's time to find that special someone because it's too many diseases and gold digging ho's out here.

"Ugh. I guess my sex is nothing compared to theirs." She seemed offended.

"I would never compare you to anyone, anyway. I do want you to do me like that again." She laughed.

"I'm serious. Where did you learn how to make love to a guy?" I now had her against the door waiting on an answer. I could hear everyone inside laughing and talking shit.

"I don't know. I'm a homebody so I watch a lot of television. Porn is ok but erotica is better because it's passionate. It makes you feel like they're in love and they'll do anything to please their lover."

"Damn." I stared at her and she was serious as hell. What woman at the age of nineteen even thought about shit like that?

"Who said we're having sex again anyway? We are about to be parents, that's it."

"Yea ok. I want you to know the day you told me it wasn't my kid, I told my mom."

"Such a mamas boy."

"I am and proud of it. Anyway, I'm going to request a DNA."

"I understand and I'm not offended. I was being reckless so it is, what it is." I opened the door and everyone stopped talking.

"What?" I asked.

"It's about damn time the two of you spoke. Y'all were

50

getting on my nerves." Zariah said and Gabby threw a plastic cup at her that was sitting on the table.

"We'll be back." AJ said.

"Where y'all going?"

"Up the street to the bar. Call when you ready to go to the airport. You coming Gabby?" Brea asked.

"No." I answered for her.

"Well damn nigga. Gabby has a mouth." James Jr. said laughing and walking out the door.

"Whatever. Lock the door." I took Gabby's hand in mine and led her to my room.

She started helping me put my clothes in totes. I'm glad I'm able to bring all this back on my family's jet without anyone checking. Otherwise, I would have had to send it in a bunch of boxes. She asked if I wanted the stuff in the kitchen but I didn't need any of those things. My mom put the house on the market and told the real estate lady they could have everything in it. I know whoever purchased it would be happy as hell.

"You, Morgan and my mom are all pregnant together."

"Your mom."

"Yea. She made a bet with my aunt Hazel years ago that she'd get to ten kids before her but my aunt stopped at six."

"Wow. Ten kids."

"Yup. My dad wouldn't leave her alone until she gave him ten. He told her she should've never made the bet." We both started laughing.

"Your parents are like mine. My dad would do anything for her."

"Yea, that's pretty much my dad and if you come for my mom, he'll make you wish you were never born." I could see the nervousness in her face. I put the tote down and walked over to her.

"Don't look like that. My mom is a sweetheart and she will have your back before mine if she likes you. Morgan can do no wrong in my moms eyes and MJ gets mad as hell when she runs to her." I lifted her chin and placed my lips on hers.

"Mmmmm Alex. I don't think we should take it there. You have a girlfriend and I don't want any problems." She said and continued allowing me to remove her shirt.

"If you want me, she's gone. I told you that before." I kissed her again and unsnapped her bra.

"I miss these." I caressed both of them and stopped. I shut the bedroom door because there's no telling when everyone will come back. She put some music on her phone and put it on the dresser.

"Where was I?" She jumped in my arms and put her hand on the back of my head.

"Alex, I don't want you to go back to her. I want you." I smiled and looked at her as she laid in my bed naked. I took my shirt off and kissed down her body until I made it to my new best friend.

"Sssssssss Alex."

"You like this Gabby?" I sucked on her nub and let go; teasing her.

"Yesssss. Shit." I opened her legs wider and went back to pleasing her.

"Alex, I'm cumming babyyyyyyy." Her cream gushed out and I drank it up like it was the last juice in the house.

"I want you too Gabby." I told her and slid inside her slow. I remember how much it hurt her when we had sex the first time. I'm not cocky at all but my dad definitely blessed me with a good ten inches.

"But you're leaving. Oh my gawdddd. I'm cumming again Alex."

"You can come with me." She stared at me. Her facial expressions were turning me on even more. Every time I hit her g-spot she'd close her eyes. If I dug deep, she'd bite her lip and when she was cumming, her mouth would form an O and she would moan very loud, like she is now.

"Get on top." After she calmed down after the last orgasm, I helped her get on and she did her thing.

"Fuck Gabby. I want you with me. I need to be in this pussy everyday. Shitttt." She smiled looking down and fucked me so good, I didn't want to move. We ended up going two rounds before we stopped and jumped in the shower. We tried to get out so no one knew what we did, but it didn't work out that way.

"I see you two perverts made up." Zariah said slurring

at her words. She didn't drink a lot because of school, but when she did it was funny.

"Whatever." Gabby walked past us and all of a sudden glass started shattering and everyone hit the floor.

Bullets were coming too fast for any of us to fire back. After about five minutes, the shooting stopped and I say five minutes because that's what it felt like. I turned Gabby over to make sure she was ok. She was shaken up a bit but fine. Brea stood up and so did everyone else, except Zariah.

"Zariah drunk ass passed out." Brea said. After a few seconds of her not moving, DJ ran over and turned her over and there was a lot of blood.

"Oh my God! Zariah wake up." Brea was now screaming and kneeling down in front of her.

"Somebody check outside and make sure its clear. I have to get my sister to a hospital." I ran outside behind AJ and James to check. We yelled to bring her out and Darius helped him.

"Brea lets go." Mateo tried to get her to move but she didn't.

Zariah was her best friend and I think she was in shock. He picked her up and carried her to the car. All of us hopped in and I had to make the dreadful call to my cousin. I looked back as we pulled off and the house looked like something out of a gangsta movie. There were so many bullet holes; it's a wonder only Zariah was hit.

"Heaven, its Alex." I said in the phone when she answered.

"What's up baby? I made your favorite food."

"Heaven, something happened to Zariah and-"

"What happened to her?" I felt a few tears coming down my face. Zariah was my favorite cousin and to see what happened to her, had me breaking down.

"Alex, what happened to Zariah?" I heard big Dayquan say. He must've snatched the phone from her. Gabby took the phone from me.

"Hi Mr. Martin. This is Gabby. You should get to the hospital. DJ has her and its best you get there as soon as you can." I heard her say a few more things and hang the phone up. I appreciated that because I couldn't speak at the moment.

"She' s going to be fine Alex." Just then my phone started ringing and it was MJ.

"Yea."

"Are you good? I'm on my way."

"The jet is here MJ. I was supposed to come back but.-"

"That's not a factor right now Alex. I'm coming to you and so is the family. You already know we make it happen. How's Zariah?"

"I don't know. They're in the car ahead of us."

"Alright listen. I have four carloads of security already there waiting for you guys at the emergency department. Once you go in the hospital, it will be on lock down so make sure everyone is there before you walk in. Heaven and Dayquan are on the way so wait for them too."

"Pull up the camera from your phone and see if you can tell who it is. We just got here." I told him and gave the code to access everything.

I guess the dude we killed last week wasn't lying when he said someone in Jersey was after us too. I sent Gabby in and had her call Akeem, who was there before us so she didn't have to. AJ must've called him in the car.

"Is she ok Alex?" I heard Heaven running up behind me. Zariah is her miracle baby. She went through a lot between the guy before big Dayquan and never thought she could carry. When she popped up pregnant with her, she was a miracle as she says.

"I don't know. We were all at the house chilling. They had just come from the bar and someone shot the house up. Heaven we thought she was drunk on the ground until DJ turned her over. We had no idea she was hit and there was a lot of blood." She covered her mouth and ran inside.

"Lock it down." I told the guy MJ said was in charge and watched him send four people to the door and next thing I heard over the intercom, was the hospital saying it was on lock down and people are not to panic because it will be lifted shortly. Damn, my family is the shit.

Akeem

When AJ called to tell me something happened to Zariah, I had just gotten out the shower. I planned a perfect night for us because a nigga was about to propose and give her what she wanted the most, and that was a kid. I knew how bad Zariah wanted a baby. I was holding out because I got some shit going on in my life, plus she's in med school. It's extremely hard to be a doctor; especially a black one and she didn't need any distractions.

I got to the hospital at the same time my cousin pulled up with her and it was a lot of blood. No one told me what happened, as of yet and now we're all sitting here waiting for the doctor to come out and tell us something.

Two hours passed by, but it felt more like ten. Her mom was hysterical and her pops and brothers were like madmen on the phone trying to figure out who did it. Alex stayed on the phone with his brother and AJ and the rest of the guys were sitting there waiting with me.

I had to get Alex to go by the door just to let my mom and dad in. My mom loved her some Zariah and I'm sure it was killing her too. She gave me a hug and they went over to speak to Zariah parents. I went to the bathroom and answered my phone in there to keep everyone out my conversation. Bad enough I'm in this shit now.

"It's time."

"So. I told you to call me when it's done."

"Akeem, you say it likes it's a job."

"It is. I didn't want this, you did."

"Too bad now." She hung up and sent me a text telling me where to meet her. I walked out the bathroom and AJ stood there shaking his head.

"Tell me you had nothing to do with this." He whispered trying to keep quiet.

"With what?" He pointed to Zariah's family.

"HELL NO!! I shouted making everyone look.

"You know I planned on asking her to marry me tonight. Why would you even ask me some shit like that?" I pushed past him and he grabbed my arm.

"I heard you on the phone cuz."

"AJ. Trust me. It's not what you think at all. I got in

60

some shit and it's coming back to bite me in the ass." I punched the vending machine so hard the glass broke.

"Yo what's up? We need to handle somebody." James Jr. came over asking.

"Nah I'm good. Just pissed off that someone is trying this family." My phone went off and it was her again, begging me to come. My mom saw the look on my face and came to where I was.

"Let's take a walk." I told her and she swooped her arm in mine as we rode the elevator up to the third floor. She gave me a crazy look but didn't say anything. I asked for the chick's room and walked in to see her crack head mom and piece of shit brother. I couldn't stand him and beat his ass one day with my cousin over Gabby. Tara looked at me and I walked out and asked the nurse to come in.

"Can I get an emergency DNA test done?" Tara had a smirk on her face while my mom stood there with no reaction whatsoever.

****

I wanted to go downstairs to check on Zariah but I was

61

too nervous this dumb bitch would have the results changed. My mom kept shaking her head and my dad, who my mom called up, took me in the hallway and cursed my ass out. Everyone knew how much Zariah meant to me but if this baby is mine; she'll never take me back.

Tara asked me several times if I wanted to hold the kid and each time I told her no. I refused to get attached to a child that wasn't mine or by Zariah. My mom did peek at him. She never said a word but he must be mine because off the bat, she would've said it wasn't.

AJ called my phone a few times and I kept sending him to voicemail. I finally sent a text and asked him to come up here. I couldn't leave but I needed to know if Zariah was ok.

Unfortunately, he came with James, Gabby and Alex, who made everything ten times worse. Once PJ's stupid ass saw his ex with Alex, he started popping mad shit. Alex put him to sleep on the ground and Gabby walked in the room. She saw Tara and asked whose baby was it and why didn't she call her.

They were close because of her brother but not close

enough to know about us. When she told Gabby I was the father, Alex walked away shaking his head. Gabby stayed with me because she is my cousin but James Jr. left too. I was hoping neither of them said anything but being they were tight, I'm sure he did as soon as he got down there.

"Akeem please tell me Tara is lying. I know you don't have a kid. Especially since Zariah had asked you numerous times to give her one." Gabby made it sound worse when it came out like that.

"It wasn't like that, but it's a possibility. We're waiting on the results now."

"Oh my God Akeem. This is going to kill Zariah. How could you?" Gabby eyes looked like they were about to let some tears fall.

"I know man."

We sat up there for hours waiting and come to find out the kid is mine. My mom started crying for Zariah. She knew it was over between us and nothing was going to make her take me back. I'm not even going to front; I shed my own tears for my girl. I thought about how I got myself in this stupid ass situation.

Tara and I met last year when I picked her and Gabby up from a party. I was fucked up and really had no business driving. Zariah and I were on a break because she was mad I wouldn't have sex with her raw and here I slept with this random chick that way with no problem. Anyway, I dropped my cousin off at home and then Tara, because she lived a few streets over from me.

She hopped in the front and started feeling on my leg and moving up to my dick. Of course, I moved her hand and told her I'm good. I turned on her street and shorty had her head in my lap sucking my dick. I lifted her up but she wouldn't stop and I fell victim to that bomb ass head.

Instead of parking in front of her house, I pulled down the street where you could barely see and let her finish. After I came in her mouth, my head was on the seat relaxing as I tried to come down off the high. I felt her climb on top of me and I tossed her off but she didn't get far.

She hopped out the car and ran to the driver side. She opened the door and her hand stroked my dick to life. She

64

jumped on my lap and slid down. I should've made her get up

but I didn't. I fucked her for over an hour in my car and

regretted it after.

I took Tara home and never spoke to her again. I went straight to the doctors and got checked the next day. I knew Zariah and I would be together again and wanted to make sure I didn't give her anything. A month later, we got back together and neither of us discussed what we did on the break. I knew what she did but I'm sure she had no idea about me. It didn't even dawn on me to come clean about sleeping with Tara because her having my kid, never crossed my mind.

Two weeks ago, I run into this stupid bitch telling me she got pregnant that night. She claims she didn't know but I'm sure it's a lie. I would've taken her straight to the clinic, had I known. I was reckless as hell for sleeping with another woman raw, that I knew nothing about.

I went downstairs to check on Zariah and everyone gave me a dirty look. I stood by AJ, who had a disgusted look on his face too.

"Let me talk to you." Big Dayquan said and walked

with me outside. Her mom and aunt Violet came too. I didn't even know Alex's parents were here yet but being upstairs all night, I guess they slipped in.

"Did you have a kid with someone else?" He asked.

"Yes." Heaven and Violet both covered their mouth and her pops jacked me up against the wall.

"You cheated on my daughter. What type of fuck shit you on? I told you never to hurt her. Didn't I?"

"Yo, what the fuck?" I heard my pops shout when he saw the gun pointed at me.

"Fuck all that. Your son did some foul shit to my daughter and he's about to pay for it."

"I don't give a fuck what he did. Take that fucking gun out his face."

"Nah. I can't do that. He's about to take a-".

"Dayquan stop. This isn't going to solve anything." Heaven said pushing him back. He still had the gun pointed at me.

"Get the fuck out of here and don't come back." He yelled when he saw everyone coming out.

"You can be mad all you want, but don't ever pull your shit out on my son. I'm his father and if it's a problem, I'm right here." My dad handed my mom his stuff and they were getting ready to square up.

"Calm the fuck down." We heard and it was big Miguel.

"Steel, you're my man and I understand you standing up for your son but I think it's best if you and your family leave."

"Not a problem." He walked behind me to make sure nothing would happen.

"Lets go Gabby." My uncle Aiden yelled. I turned around and saw her let Alex hand go and felt bad. I knew they really liked each other but she's my blood, so fuck it.

"Gabby really!"

"Alex, please don't make me choose. I know what my cousin did is wrong but he's my blood."

"It's all good. You know what?" He got closer to her.

"Don't hit my line until you have the baby. Once we get it tested, and if it's mine, I'm taking it."

"HOLD THE FUCK UP!" Now my uncle Aiden was pissed.

67

"Don't do it Aiden." Big Miguel said stepping in front of Alex. Guns were drawn on both sides and everything.

"I don't give a fuck how big your family is. Your son ain't about to disrespect my daughter because she chose her family the same way he did. Fuck out of here with that."

"Again. Aiden, I have no issues with your family and being it may be extended soon, let's keep it that way. As far as my son, my wife and I will deal with him. Have a good night."

"Yea alright. What the fuck ever?" He grabbed Gabby's hand and Arizona's and walked to their car. I felt bad for AJ because he had his gun drawn against them and DJ is his best friend.

Gabby

"Who the fuck do he think he is?" My uncle was yelling, as he and my dad stood in the kitchen drinking a beer. I don't blame them or Akeem. Yea, he was wrong for having a kid on Zariah but none of us knew. We all know how he felt about her so something must've happened for him to have a kid by someone else. However, her dad should've never pulled a gun on my cousin either.

"Akeem how could you have a kid with someone else?" My aunt asked. He told us that they were on a break and weren't even speaking. He slept with Tara the night he brought us home from a party and that was it. After he got back with Zariah he never cheated. I could ask why sleep with someone else when he knew they'd get back together but after three months, I'd assume it was really over too.

I could see how conflicted my brother was and Brea couldn't stop crying. She cried for her friend and the fact her father and uncle were almost shot. We were outnumbered like crazy so to think they would've survived, is crazy. I sat by her and laid my head on her lap. Mateo called her phone over and over but she shut it off.

"Well all we can do is, say fuck them and take care of my grandson." Steel said walking in the living room and stood behind Phoenix.

"You good nephew? I know he's your best friend and I would never tell you to choose but as you can see, he did." My brother didn't say a word.

"I'm over the shit. Gabby, I don't want you anywhere around them. And before you even think about opening your mouth, don't. You may be grown but you're still my daughter."

"I know dad. I agree that it's best to stay away." AJ looked at me.

"I'm sorry AJ but I choose family. Yes, theirs is much bigger but we're all we got. Never mind Alex threatened to take my baby."

"Gabby you know he was mad."

"Wait a fucking minute." My mom went in my brothers' face. She never curses or get upset but she was pissed.

"I know good and well you're not making an excuse for the way he spoke to your sister."

"Ma, I'm saying." He stood up and my father pulled my mom back and was in his face.

"You may be grown, but I will knock you the fuck out if you ever stand in your mothers face like that again."

"Pops, I wasn't trying to get in her face. I-"

"I don't give a fuck what you thought." My brother was pissed my dad was in his face and balled his fist up. *Wrong move!*

"Oh you wanna fight? Come on nigga. You tough. You rather have those motherfuckers back then your own family." My dad punched him in the ribs and AJ hunched over.

"Daddy stop."

"Aiden please stop. I don't want my husband and son fighting. He didn't mean it."

"Nah. It's about time these young niggas see what it's like to fight a man and not pull out a gun. Come on AJ." He went to hit him again and my mom jumped in the way and he ended up hitting her and she fell back. He had caught her on

71

the side of her face.

"Oh my God." Me, my aunt and Brea ran over to my mom who had blood coming from her eye. AJ rushed my dad and fell on top of him and punched him a few times. My dad flipped him over and started fucking my brother up. AJ tried his best to block his hits but my dad landed all of them. My uncle and Akeem finally got him off. AJ stood up and started talking shit.

"I love you ma, but I'm out."

"AJ please don't leave." I tried to get him to stay but he wasn't hearing it.

"I'll talk to you later Gabby."

"That's right punk ass motherfucker, run to them. Bitch ass nigga."

"AJ please tell me that's not where you're going."

"Ma, DJ asked me to bring him some stuff and-" my mom waved her hand at him. His facial expression changed from angry to sad. He was hurting my mom and now I was pissed.

"I HATE YOU AJ. LOOK WHAT YOU'RE DOING

TO OUR FAMILY!"

"Gabby." He tried to touch me.

"GET OUT AJ. I CHOSE MY FAMILY OVER MY KIDS' FATHER. YOU HEARD HIM SPEAK TO ME AS IF I WERE NOTHING. OUR FATHERS ALMOST FOUGHT AND YOU'RE STILL ON THEIR SIDE. GET OUT!" I started punching him in the chest over and over until I felt someone move me.

"Ma." AJ yelled out but my mom refused to look at him. My dad lifted her up and carried her upstairs. All he kept saying was sorry and he didn't mean it. I felt bad for him because we knew it was an accident.

"AJ, I'm sorry you're caught up in this and I know it's hard, but really." Brea said.

"Did you not just watch my father beat my ass? Huh? Y'all sitting here yelling at me for having my friends back when my own family is turning against me. What am I supposed to do?"

"No one is turning against you AJ. You asked for that ass whooping trying to be tough. You know how daddy is

73

when it comes to our mom."

"You know I would never disrespect my mother." He said trying to make himself believe it.

"The moment you step outside this house to go tend to them, you are. I mean for God's sake AJ, your mom tried to protect you from your dad, got hurt in the process, and you're still leaving. Do you even care how much its hurting her?" My aunt Phoenix asked him.

"At least none of them will call me all types of bitch ass niggas and try to fight me. Fuck all y'all." My uncle ran up on AJ but Phoenix stepped in front of him.

"Get your ungrateful ass the fuck out my house. You want to be a part of their family so bad, then have at it." AJ put up his two fingers and said peace. My uncle slammed the door and walked up to his room.

I ran up the steps to check on my mom, who was in the guest room and Brea was right behind me. My dad was lying on his back while my mom was on his chest crying and holding an ice pack to her face. Stress was written all over their faces. If I could erase what just happened, I would. I climbed in bed with my mom and so did Brea. Thank goodness it was a king sized bed, otherwise we would be super tight.

"I'm terminating my pregnancy." Her and my dad sat up.

"No Gabby."

"It's too much dealing with their family and I can't take the chance of them taking my baby. They have so much power and I'm scared."

"Gabby, do not get rid of the baby. I'm not worried about them. They scare others but ain't no fear over here." I loved how my dad wasn't scared of them but I didn't want him fighting my battles.

"Gabby, someone is here to see you." Phoenix said when she opened the door. I wiped my face and went downstairs to see Violet and Joy sitting in the living room. How the fuck did they know I was here.

"Hello Gabriela. I'm Violet and this is my daughter Joy. I'm sorry we didn't meet under better circumstances." I offered them a seat on the couch.

"I'm sure you know why I'm here." I sat down across

from her. She was indeed a gorgeous woman and so is her daughter.

"I'm not sure I do." Brea sat next to me.

"I'm not here to apologize for Alex because that's his shit. I just came to tell you, that if the baby is his, we would like to be in his or her life." I chuckled a little.

"Mrs. Rodriquez, I'm sorry you wasted your time coming here but I've decided to terminate my pregnancy." Her and Joy looked at one another.

"Don't you think my brother should be allowed to make that decision with you?" Joy asked and I could tell she was aggravated. This time I laughed.

"For what? He already thinks this baby isn't his, so who cares if I get rid of it. Yea, I threw it out there because I was mad, but to be honest, Alex and I are young and not fit to be parents."

"You should've thought of that before you-"

"No disrespect Mrs. Rodriquez, but don't come into my aunts house and think because you and your husband run shit, that you can run me."

76

"Who you talking to bitch?" Joy said and stood up. Brea was now on her feet.

"I'm a bitch. You don't even know me."

"You're right and I don't care to. If that's my niece or nephew, then that's all I'm worried about. You think you're tough but I'll fuck you up and won't give it a second thought." I closed my eyes and tried to calm down. This heffa thought I was scared of her and because I'm pregnant, it's the only reason I won't offer her to go outside.

"Calm down Joy. Let her finish." Her mom said making her sit back down.

"As I was saying. Your son is not the guy I met months ago. He is an arrogant, controlling asshole and when he doesn't get his way, tries to make a person feel like shit. Well guess what, my parents raised me to never let a man treat me like shit."

"I'm sorry but wasn't your last boyfriend whooping that ass?" Joy said and smirked.

"He did lay hands on me a few times but you live and you learn. What I won't do is allow your brother to do it. I mean it does run in the family." Mrs. Rodriquez was so quick, I didn't see it coming.

The punch to my face hurt like a motherfucker. My mom came out of nowhere and punched her in the face. Before they could fight, my dad snatched her up and my uncle got his mom. Joy had a gun pointed at my mom and I lost it

I jumped on top of her and started punching her in the face. She flipped me over and it was no winning after that. Once she banged my head in the ground that was it. . Everyone was still yelling over what happened between our moms, they didn't even realize we were fighting.

"What the fuck?" I heard Alex's voice. He lifted his sister up and tossed her on the couch. Our moms were arguing and big Miguel came through the door with a scary look on his face. His security was deep as hell. The entire scene was crazy. He looked at his wife, daughter and then at me.

"In a situation like this, I would terminate all you motherfuckers for fucking with my family, but it looks like I don't have to. What you just lost will haunt your family enough, to satisfy my need to kill you." He pointed to me and I looked down to see blood running down my legs. It was all over my shoes and seeping through my jeans. I didn't even notice until he mentioned it.

"Gabby no." My mom yelled and ran over to me. I stood there with tears racing down my face. Alex stared at me with his own falling.

"Gabby." He tried to come near me but I put my arm out. I could feel the blood gushing out, well my baby.

"No Alex. This is the second time in one night your family has come for mine. Your mom punched me in the face, so yes, my mom hit her. She's supposed to, I'm her daughter and she had every right to defend me. Then your favorite sister here, pulled a gun on my mom and yes I hit her, to protect my mom." I could see Miguel shaking his head at both of them. The look Alex gave Joy is one I never want to see him give me.

"You wanted me to choose at the hospital and I didn't, which made them come here and now look. My baby is gone. OUR BABY IS DEAD ALEX. YOUR SISTER KILLED MY BABY."

"Gabby. You need to get to the hospital."

"For what Alex? I can feel my baby's spirit leaving my body. I HATE YOU. I FUCKING HATE YOU."

"Gabby, I'm.-" I heard his sister say.

"Don't you fucking dare let those words leave your mouth." I gave her the most evil glare I could.

"You wanted to know if this was your baby right. Well here's some blood for you to take a DNA. Here take both of them." I took my shoes off and threw it at him. Everyone remained quiet.

"Gabby, I know it was my baby."

"It doesn't even matter anymore Alex. Just go." I dropped to the floor grabbing my stomach. I guess with my adrenaline pumping, I didn't feel the pain in the beginning but now it was full force.

"Let me take you.-"

"JUST GO!!!! STAY AWAY FROM ME. YOU AND YOUR FAMILY ARE HATEFUL PEOPLE. YOU TERRORIZE FAMILIES WITH YOUR POWER. I DON'T EVER WANT TO SEE YOU AGAIN. DAD CAN YOU

TAKE ME UPSTAIRS?" My father came over, lifted me up and took me in the room. My mom came in the bathroom with me and so did my aunt. They helped me peel my clothes off and made me take a shower.

It was so much blood that the bottom of the shower was red. I heard my dad yell through the door that a doctor would be by in fifteen minutes to check on me. Once I got out, my mom laid a few towels on the bed so when the doctor checked me I wouldn't mess up the sheets. Brea came in and laid with me, but all I wanted was my dad. He came in and got in bed with me.

"I know I said I would get rid of it, but I wasn't daddy. I wanted my baby." I said when he came in after the doctor left. I was now hysterically crying.

"I know Gabby. I know."

I can't believe me and my pops were fighting. Well, he was beating my ass but I got some hits in. I felt bad for my sister because we were close and after what happened, I'm sure she'll never speak to me again. I wanted to stay and make sure my mom was ok but the way everyone was feeling, it was best to leave.

I stopped by DJ's and grabbed a few bricks and some trees. I made a stop at the trap house to check things out and picked up some wraps from seven eleven. I got back to the hospital and it seemed like everyone was gone except DJ and his parents.

We found out Zariah got hit in the chest and grazed on her neck before we left. They still had her down in the recovery room right now until they had a room for her. I went outside with DJ and we sat in the car smoking in silence. Both of our phones started going off at the same time. I opened up my text and almost dropped the blunt.

Brea: *You're so quick to call them your family. Well guess what? Your bitch Joy came over with her mother and* *fought your sister. Gabby lost the baby asshole.* She had a bunch of mad faces after the text.

"I got to go bro. I'll hit you up later."

"All right." He got out the car without our normal handshake and slammed the door. I was over everyone's attitude. I drove to my house and saw Joy sitting on my porch crying.

"What are you doing here?" I walked right past her to unlock my door.

"I'm sorry AJ. I didn't mean to fight her but she got smart with my mom, then my mom hit her." She went on and on and told me everything that went down. I felt like shit because I couldn't be there for my family. I sent my sister a text and told her I'm sorry and if she needs me to call.

"I'll be back." I left her sitting on my couch and went to take a shower. My ribs were killing me and I probably needed a doctor but oh well. If I'm moving, I'm good.

"I'm sorry AJ." I turned around and Joy was in the shower with me naked.

"Joy what are you doing?"

"What we both want." She pulled my head to her and kissed me. I sucked on her neck and then moved down to her breasts. Her hands were on my head as I went lower and found her pretty ass pussy. Not a razor bump, or scratch anywhere.

"Mmmmm." You taste good baby." I stared at her as I felt her pearl growing in my mouth. I lifted her right leg on my shoulder and stuck two fingers in. She jumped a little and I looked up at her. I know damn well she ain't a virgin. I stood up, turned the shower off and carried her in the bedroom.

I laid her down and let my mouth make love to her pussy again. After she came a few times, I kissed up her body, grabbed a condom out my nightstand and placed the tip at her tunnel. She wrapped her arms around me to kiss and I tried to push my way through but it was hard. She let some tears fall down her face and I stopped.

"How could you not mention you're a virgin?" I saw some blood on the condom and shook my head.

"I didn't want you to say no." I tossed it in the toilet.

"Joy your virginity is not something you can't get back."

"I know AJ but I'm giving it to you because I want to." She stood in front of me and climbed in my lap.

"Joy this isn't-" she put her tongue in my mouth and wrapped her legs around my waist. I lifted her up and placed her down on the bed. I was in the exact same position, forcing my way in again. The further I got, the better it felt. I kissed her tears away and went slow as possible. Not too long after, she was so wet; I had to stop so I wouldn't cum.

"Is it true that if a woman does this she can make a man cum?" She squeezed her pussy muscles on my dick and I damn sure came.

"Fuckkkkkk Joy." I held her still. She leaned in to kiss me.

"I guess it is." She sucked on my bottom lip and grinded on top, to get me hard.

"Come take a shower with me." I helped her get up and she could barely walk. We stepped in the shower and she lathered the rag up and washed both of our bodies.

"AJ can I try this?" I was getting ready to shut the water off.

"Try what?"

"Joyyyyyyy." I moaned out when she put me in her mouth.

"Damn girl. You doing that shit real good." I let my head fall against the shower wall. Joy had my balls in her mouth and jerked me at the same time. It felt so fucking good; I tried to lift her before I came.

"I like the way you taste baby." She kissed up my body.

"You sucked dick before." I had her by the back of her neck staring up at me. I felt some kind of way. If I was her first, I should've been at everything.

"No AJ. You're the only man I've done that to or had sex with."

"Has anyone eaten my pussy?" Hell yea, I was claiming it. I'm going to be her first and last.

"My ex. But he was no where near as good as you."

"Oh yea. Turn around." I spread her legs apart, put her arms on the shower wall and rammed inside her.

"Ahhhhhhh." She screamed out. I kissed her spine and

86

put my hands on hers as I whispered in her ear.

"No other nigga better not ever taste…" I pounded inside her.

"Smell..." I pounded a little harder.

"Or fuck my pussy again. Do you understand?" I hit her with one so deep she started to shake.

"Yea baby, let that pussy cum. Damn it looks good."

I turned her around and lifted one leg in the crook of my arm and continued to beat the pussy up. For it to be her first time, she did a good job hanging in there."

"I love you AJ." I stared at her, and then attacked her mouth.

"I love you too Joy. Fuckkkkkkk, this pussy so good. I'm cumming again." We both stood there panting hard.

"Let me wash you up this time." I washed us up and carried her in the room to lie down. I had to sit her on the chair first and change the sheets. I definitely popped her cherry.

She ended up falling straight to sleep but I ordered us something to eat anyway. I figured if she woke up hungry, there would be food. I went downstairs to wait for it to come.

My phone was on the table vibrating. It was a message from my sister saying leave her alone. I had to make up with my family. Shit is getting crazy out here and honestly, I miss them already.

After the food came, I ate a little and took some up to Joy but she told me to let her sleep. I laughed because she had no idea I was about to wake her up for some more. I made sure my house was locked up and got some more of that good pussy.

Over the next few days all Joy and I did was eat, sleep and fuck. We tried to watch a movie, but a part where they would have sex came on, and we did the same. I kept asking if she was sore, and she said yes but that she's going home in a few days so she'll deal with it. As long as her pussy stayed wet; I wasn't complaining.

****

"AJ open up." I heard as me and Joy were lying on the couch. I tapped her to get up so I could get the door.

"WHAT?" I snatched it open. I knew it was Shayla from her voice.

"AJ why aren't you talking to me anymore?"

"You know why." She came barging in and Joy sat up smirking.

"Really. You left me alone for her? She left you after the accident and-"

"Because you lied and said you was my girl. I broke up with you weeks before my accident. Then you fucked me as I woke up, knowing how weak I was and couldn't fight you off."

"AJ you had me suck you off. You were aware."

"I did because you wouldn't get up so I said fuck it. Then you jumped on me again."

"Are you pregnant?" Joy asked walking towards her. Shayla smirked and lifted her shirt. At this very moment I wanted to beat the shit out of her. I pushed her out the door.

"If the kid is mine, I'll take care of him and only him. You won't get shit out of me so don't even try." I slammed the door in her face. I was pissed and knocked everything off my table.

"AJ I'm not upset. She's foul as hell for what she did but all you can do is get a test and take care of the baby." There was another knock at the door and Joy went to answer it, in just my T-shirt.

"Where's my brother?" I heard Gabby's voice. I guess she changed her mind about not speaking to me.

"You ok?" She smacked the shit out of me.

"How dare you lay up with the bitch who killed my baby?"

"Don't put your hands on me again." She sucked her teeth and stood there with an attitude. I think she wanted me to make Joy leave.

"Gabby, I know you don't have shit to say to me and you probably look at me like the scum of the earth but I really am sorry. I never meant to make you lose the baby. If I could take it back-"

"But you can't, can you? My baby is gone because you and your hideous family couldn't leave well enough alone. Your brother is a dick, your mom and dad-"

"Watch it Gabby. I may have apologized and you don't have to accept it. However, I'm not disrespecting your family and I would appreciate it if you didn't put my family in it. You can call me all the names you want, we can fight again but leave them out of it."

"Come in here Gabby." I grabbed her and she tried to fight me. I took her upstairs in one of the guest rooms and shut the door. She kept pushing me out the way to leave.

"I'm sorry sis. I'm sorry for fighting with our parents, for making you angry and most of all, for not being there when you lost the baby." She dropped to the ground and started crying harder. I hugged her until she calmed down. We both sat on the floor with our backs against the bed. Her head was on my shoulder and my head was on hers.

"How could you choose them over us?"

"I didn't choose anyone. Yes, I was fucked up over what happened but it's never been them."

"But you left."

"Pops was going to kill me Gabby. He thought I stepped to mom and had uncle Steel and Akeem not gotten him off me, I'd probably be laid up in the hospital." She laughed.

"You made him hit mommy. Daddy is so hurt over what he did to her and barely speaks. Mommy keeps telling him she's fine but all he thinks about is what if she had a seizure or hit the floor too hard. He's going through it AJ." I ran my hand down my face. I forgot all about my moms' health issues. Now I see why my pops was so mad. Anything could trigger her seizures; including stress.

"I have to see her."

"AJ, daddy is not going to let you around her. You'll have to go through him first. You know how overprotective he is of her and he won't take any chances on you upsetting her."

"I know." I heard a knock on the door.

"I'm going to go. Gabby, I really am sorry." My sister didn't even acknowledge her.

"I'll be right back." I went outside to the car she was driving and kneeled down.

"You coming back."

"Do you want me to?"

"What kind of question is that?" She shrugged her shoulders.

"Joy, I don't go around telling women I love them, sleep with them for a few days and not speak again. You are my woman now, so yes I expect to see you later. I'll leave the key under the rug for you, just in case you come and I'm out."

"I'm sorry for what happened AJ."

"Stop Joy. You said it enough. If she doesn't accept it, you can't make her." She nodded her head.

"I love you AJ."

"I love you too. Text me when you get to where you're going." I kissed her and went in the house.

"Are you in love with her?" Gabby was sitting in the living room with her feet folded on the couch.

"Yup." I plopped down and looked at the television. We both stayed in that same spot for hours until she was ready to go. I gave her a hug and told her I would see her tomorrow. I had to make things right with my parents.

Zariah

I opened my eyes and noticed my parents, DJ and almost my entire family. The only person I didn't see, was my man. My dad realized I was awake first and ran over to me. Then my mom came kissing all over me. She tells everyone I'm her miracle baby. I tried to wipe her eyes but the pain in my chest was excruciating and I felt some bandages on my neck.

"Where's Akeem?" I asked and no one said a word. My aunt and Joy told me they had somewhere to be and would see me later.

"Um, he was here but we sent him home." My dad said and everyone stepped out.

"Why would you do that?" My mom grabbed my hand and kissed the back of it.

"Honey. Did he ever cheat on you?" I gave her the side eye the best I could. Why would she be asking me this?

"I'm asking because honey, he ugh… well we just found out… Day you tell her." My father was mad she put it on him.

"I'm sorry Zariah but some chick gave birth to his son yesterday." The air left my body when he said it.

"Excuse me." I had to make him repeat it. There's no way he said what I think he said.

"We were in the waiting room and he took his mom upstairs. He called AJ and asked him to come up; only he brought his sister, your cousin Alex and JJ. The test was handed to him and he is indeed the baby's father." I felt the tears coming down my face and I saw my brother DJ and my other brother James, who my mom named after her dad, standing there with evil looks on their face.

I laid there full of hurt and anger. How could he have a child with another woman, when I've been asking him for years to give me one? There had to be some sort of mistake with the test because he wouldn't do me like that.

"Call him up here."

"Zariah, why don't you wait until you feel better?"

"I can't wait that long. I need to know now. Mommy can you please call him up here." I saw her type away on her phone and she told me he said ok. I asked them to stand outside when he came but not to leave. I would need the support if what they were telling me turned out to be true. It's not that I didn't believe them, but I wanted him to tell me to my face.

We were talking about what happened with me when he walked in. I could see the sad look and knew it was true, yet, I still asked.

"Is it true?" My family stood up and walked out. DJ bumped him on the way.

"Zariah listen."

"IS IT TRUE?" I asked in a stern voice trying not to yell. He leaned against the wall and put his head on it.

"Yes. It happened when you broke up with me. I was high and had been drinking. I gave Gabby and her friend a ride home. We dropped my cousin off first, she hopped in the front seat and one thing led to another."

"Why Akeem? I know we were broken up but you wouldn't even give me a baby. How could you give her one without even thinking about it?"

"I promise it wasn't like that."

"What was it like? I mean how many times were you with her?"

"Just that night."

"I wanted to have your kids Akeem. All you had to do was stop using condoms if you wanted one. I guess I wasn't good enough."

"You know that's not true. You're the only woman I want to be with, have my kids and one day marry."

"If you believed what you're saying, we wouldn't be having this conversation." He sat on the side of the bed and took my hand in his.

"I'll do anything if you don't leave me. Those three months without you were torture. Please don't do it again."

"I can't tell, if you were out making babies. Get out Akeem."

"Zariah."

"Please go. I can't deal with any more hurt."

"Zariah, I'm not leaving."

"DAD!" I yelled and everyone came back in.

"Lets go son." I didn't know his dad was out there too.

But I guess after everything that took place earlier, he wouldn't let him come alone.

"ZARIAH!" He shouted. I stared and asked him to come closer. I put my hand on his face and pecked his lips.

"I love you Akeem but we are over. You had a child and I'm not sure I can ever get passed it. Regardless if we broke up or not, you should've known better."

"I love you too and I'm not letting you go. I'm going to get you back." I saw tears leaving his eyes and it made me more upset.

The machines were beeping and I could hear the nurses yelling for everyone to step out. This by far had to be one of the worst days of my life. I loved Akeem with all I had and he did something as stupid as getting another woman pregnant. How will I ever look at men the same?

****

I was able to leave the hospital two weeks after being shot and my mom didn't want me staying alone but I told her I was fine. I moved around slow but I could manage. Plus, I needed some alone time to deal with Akeem having a child on me. He called my phone damn near twenty times a day, trying to get me to talk. The text messages were just as sad reading, as I'm sure he was writing. I just couldn't bare speaking to him right now. It was too fresh and I'm slowly healing.

Today his mom and sister were coming by to visit me. They had been up to the hospital to see me but with all the hostility, they'd leave when my family came. I wasn't angry with them after finding out no one knew about the baby, not even Akeem. She contacted him two weeks before she had him and mentioned it.

I was sitting on the couch with no TV or music on thinking about my life. Why is it that the doorbell seems to ring loud as hell when its quiet. I walked over to it slow and opened it.

"Hey sweetie. How are you?" His mom asked and gave me a hug. I looked behind for Brea but she wasn't there.

"Brea has been with Gabby. Ever since she lost the baby, she's been upset."

"I cursed Joy out over that too. If I could do the same with my aunt Violet and get away with it, I would."

99

"Child. The entire situation is a mess but I'm not here for that." She sat down.

"How is your chest? And it seems like your neck is better."

"I'm good. I have to take it one day at a time."

"Zariah listen. I know Akeem did something incredibly stupid but I don't want you to stopped speaking to me. I still look at you like my daughter."

"How could he do that to me?" I broke down crying in her arms.

"Honey, it was a mistake and he has to deal with the consequences of losing you because of it. I can tell you, it had nothing to do with him not wanting you. He has been at my house everyday since you found out. However, when I bring the baby over he leaves." I looked at her.

"He is my grand baby and I'm not going to neglect him like his mother is."

"Huh?"

"Are you sure you want to hear about the baby?" I'm glad she asked.

100

"I'm ok with it." I shrugged my shoulders.

"I started bringing the baby to the house and noticed he's always shitty, dirty and his skin is dry from not having on lotion. I hate dropping him off because it's always so many people over there. I'm telling you, she got pregnant on purpose to hurt you."

"To hurt me. I don't even know who she is." His mom stared at me.

"The baby's mother is Tara." My eyes grew wide and my temper began to flare.

I hated that bitch with a passion. She was Gabby's friend through PJ. It's been plenty of times she's tried to get Gabby to take her over his mom's to see if he's there. Brea told me she's even come to her house claiming to look for Gabby.

I approached her and she said it wasn't like that. However, whenever we'd see her together, she'd give him googly eyes or say some slick shit about me not being able to handle him like she could. On two occasions, he had to keep me from beating her ass due to the disrespect. Akeem would never let me whoop her ass because she was not only younger but he said she'd never have him. I guess he was wrong about that.

"Why her?"

"I don't know Zariah but he hasn't been the same since finding out. He hasn't spoken to anyone and like I said before, he won't have anything to do with the baby." I shook my head in disgust. How could he not want to deal with his own son? One thing I didn't tolerate from a man, is him not taking care of his child. One day, I'll say something but for now, I'll keep my mouth shut.

Alex

"How are you honey?" My mom asked as I sat on the couch in her house. It has been two weeks since Gabby lost our baby. Yea, I was hurt when she said it wasn't mine but I knew it was.

"How you think I feel ma? Had y'all not gone over there, she'd still be pregnant."

"Alex, I told you, we went to ask if we could maintain a bond with the baby and things went left. Sweetie, she said she was going to terminate it anyway."

"VIOLET!" I heard my grandmother yell out. My mom moved them over here after Joy's first accident. The two people my mom didn't fuck with were my grandma and my dad.

"Look Alex. Maybe what happened was fate."

"Fate." I had to chuckle when she said that to keep from snapping.

"Sooooo, her bleeding out in front of me with my kid is fate? Huh?"

"Watch it Alex." My mom said.

"Ma, I have never disrespected you but I swear you make me want to." I could see how upset that comment made her. I was my moms' favorite so to hear me speaking to her this way is not something she's used to.

"Neither one of you had the right to go over there and then you put your hands on her."

"Alex.-"

"She may have pissed you off but she was pregnant ma. You knew Joy would jump in and then you stood there, and let my sister beat on her. Did you want her to lose the baby? I mean, I can't think of any other reason than that."

"Alex, I would never do that on purpose."

"Yea ok."

"ALEX MIGUEL RODRIQUEZ!" I heard my father shout. Yes, all our middle names are Miguel.

"Yea pops."

"I know you're hurting but don't speak to your mother that way. The person you should be mad at, is yourself for putting that girl in a position to choose. I could tell she loves you but it was fucked up for you to even assume she'd choose

104

you."

"I didn't mean to. I was mad and I called her to apologize but she never answered."

"Alex, you're still young and have a lot to learn and with that being said, never make a woman choose. She knows where her heart is and if a choice has to be made, then you let her do it willingly." I nodded my head.

"Don't think I didn't get in your mothers and sisters ass for the shit they pulled." My mom sucked her teeth. My dad gave her whatever she wanted but if she did something he didn't like or approve of, he'd let her have it. My mom would be so mad; she'd stop speaking to him.

"I'm not saying what they did was right because you lost a child but I understand why it was done."

"I do too, but ma didn't have to hit her. I'm so tired of everyone making excuses for you and Joy making me lose my kid. What they did pop was dead wrong and just because Gabby didn't allow them to treat her like shit, doesn't mean she deserved to get hit. You were about to kill her and her family over mom and Joy being in the wrong."

105

"Are you saying I shouldn't defend my family?" My dad asked standing in front of me.

"No pops. Everyone knows how you get down and they do too. However, did you expect her mom not to defend her because of who you are? Or what about Joy pulling a gun on her mother? I don't hear anyone apologizing for starting the shit over there. All I'm hearing is excuses on why they did it." I stood up mad as hell.

"There are no excuses. It happened and now.-" my mom said in a way I didn't appreciate.

"Like I said before. If you or my sister didn't go over there, we wouldn't be having this conversation." I walked to the door.

"I know what it's like to lose a child Alex."

"Exactly ma. Then you know it's a feeling that won't go away. She was a month behind you from when you lost our sibling. Which means she probably felt a few kicks and bonded with it. She had the ultrasound on her phone. I may be going through something but I can't imagine what she's dealing with and I won't, because she refuses to have anything to do with me. So thanks ma. I appreciate the help from you and Joy." I slammed the door and walked to my house, which was far as hell, but it would do me some good to get fresh air.

I thought about the night everything went down and should've handled it better. We were all bugging after finding out Akeem had a baby on my cousin, who had just gotten shot. Then our fathers and her uncle were ready to fight. I put Gabby in a fucked up predicament and I blame myself too. I called her over and over to say sorry but she turned the phone off.

Brea sent me a text telling me to hurry up and get there. Imagine my surprise when I saw my sister fighting Gabby. When my dad pointed out her losing the baby, my heart broke. It was so much blood that it seeped through her clothes and onto her shoes. She didn't want me to touch her and all I wanted to do was comfort her. She broke down and when I got in the car, I shed quite a bit of tears myself. Who would've known the first chick I impregnated would've lost it, due to my own family?

I walked by MJ's house and saw the lights on. I was going to stop in but knowing those two, they're probably having sex. I envied their relationship and hoped one day I would have the same.

"Hey you." Morgan walked out on the porch as I was on my way past.

"Hey."

"Come here." I went in the house behind her and MJ was lying on the couch.

"You good bro?" He sat up and I plopped down next to him.

"I will be when ma stops bringing it up. Every time I try and move past it, somehow she brings it up."

"You know you're her favorite so she's going to constantly check on you. Thanks babe." He said to Morgan who handed him a cup.

"Alex, I'm sorry it happened to you. Have you spoken to her?" She sat on MJ's lap.

"Nah. She doesn't want to hear from me."

"Make her. You know we're Rodriquez's. We don't take shit lying down."

"Alex, if you want to see her, then do it. Maybe once

you two speak, you can get past it. Everyone knows how you felt about her and so does she. If you love her, then I agree with your brother, you should go to her."

"You agree? That's surprising."

"Miguel, I agree with you a lot."

"Yea, when I'm in those guts."

"It's time to go. MJ you trying to go to Jersey tomorrow?"

"No."

"I am Alex. I haven't seen my parents, so I'll go with you."

"Dammit Alex. I got shit to do. Now I have to go to Jersey."

"She don't need you bro."

"Nah, but I need her and she ain't going nowhere without me."

"Awwww baby. I love you." They started kissing and being extra.

"Bye. I'll be ready by nine." MJ waved his hand for me to leave. Neither of them stopped for a breath. I locked their door and proceeded to my house. I saw Joy's car in the driveway and kept walking. I'm not in the mood to hear anything she has to say. I'm liable to smack the shit out of her, so its best I stay away.

I packed me a small bag for my trip and laid down on the bed. I opened my phone and went straight to Gabby's Instagram page. She used to post everyday but I hadn't seen anything since the accident. Today was the first time she posted and it was a photo of her, her brother and parents. The caption read, *family over everything*. I hit the like button and put my phone down. I ended up falling asleep and woke up the next day to MJ standing over top of me.

He told me to hurry up before he changed his mind. I got myself together and the three of us were on our way to Jersey. The entire ride those two got on my nerves with the lovey dovey shit. When we landed there were two SUV's parked when we got out. MJ checked to make sure the drivers were who they are supposed to be and told me to text him when I found her. Morgan kissed my cheek and told me good luck.

I called AJ and asked if he did what I asked and he told me yes. I was still cool with him even though his sister and I went through our shit. At the end of the day AJ has been a part of our family for years and none of us expected him to choose that day. DJ had a little attitude over him leaving the hospital because Zariah was still there, but MJ got in his ass over it.

I had the driver park on the opposite side of the road and hopped out. I looked around and smiled. I could see her walking through the house. She didn't have the shades closed and most of the house is made of glass anyway.

I walked up and retrieved the key from under the rug. When I got in she was sitting outside in the back. I made sure the door was locked and went out there. Her eyes were closed and she had earphones in. I bent down and kissed her lips. I thought she would jump but she wrapped her arms around me and pulled me on top of her. I can't lie; my ass was becoming aroused.

"Why are you here Alex?" She asked after I moved away.

"You won't talk or text me. I needed to make sure you

111

were ok." Just as I said it, I sent a message to MJ that I was here before he sent the damn swat team.

"Alex, I said I was going to get rid of the baby to your mom but I wasn't. I wanted our baby. I really did and now.-" she broke down crying. I put both hands on the side of her face.

"Gabriela Rowan. I don't blame you at all. You were protecting yourself and your mom."

"Yea, but we lost our first child."

"I know and it wasn't our time. Listen Gabby." She wiped her eyes and nose on her shirt.

"I love you and I want you to be my woman."

"You love me."

"Yea I do. I thought it was lust but every moment without you, made me want you more. You're the only one I think about and I don't want us to be apart any longer." Yea, I may have sounded like a bitch but when you're in love, you do what you have to, to keep your woman.

"I love you too Alex. I'm not sure about being your woman. Your mom doesn't like me and.-"

"I'm not worried about them and you shouldn't either. My mom is trying her hardest to get on my good side. Trust me, when I say she'll bend over backwards for you now."

"I don't want to go over there right now Alex. I also know you can't stay here because of the beef."

"Can I stay with you until I leave?"

"I guess so." She smiled and grabbed my hand to go inside.

"What you mean, you guess so?"

"You can only stay if you watch some movies with me."

"I'll do whatever you want Gabby."

"Oh yea. How did guy get in here?" She had her hands on her hips.

"Your brother made me a key."

"You still talk to him?"

"Why wouldn't I?" She shrugged her shoulders.

"Your brother has been a part of our family for a long time. We would never ask him to choose, which reminds me. I'm sorry for putting you in that position. I apologize for anything I put you through and from here on out I will try not to hurt you." She smiled and kissed me again.

We stayed up half the night watching movies and talking. When she got out the shower, I wanted to make love to her but I didn't want her to think that's the only reason I'm here. She laid her head on my arm and fell asleep.

I reached over to grab her cell that's was going off. I opened the message and it was from PJ asking if she could come over. He misses being in her good ass pussy. I couldn't stand this nigga and he's going to find out soon just who I am. I shut her phone off and got comfortable behind her. I'm right where I belong.

****

"Baby somebody is at the door." Gabby woke me up out my sleep. The sun was shining but shit, it was almost up when we fell asleep.

"Who knows you live her?"

"No one knows about this place but my family and they have a key." I put my jeans on, grabbed my gun and peeked out the window. I didn't see any cars and put a call out to my brother.

"Yo."

"Tell the driver to have my back when I open the door."

"What's going on Alex?" I told him and he started yelling. I got closer to the front door and pointed my gun in his face when I opened it.

"You play too fucking much." I told MJ. He brushed past me with Morgan shaking her head.

"I told him not to, but he's full of damn jokes today."

"Awww baby, don't be mad at me." He lifted Morgan on one of the barstools.

"Come on so we can go to breakfast. My wife is hungry." I sucked my teeth and went to the truck and grabbed my bag. I got upstairs and Gabby was on the phone looking nervous as hell.

"It's just my brother and his girl. Come take a shower with me. They're taking us to breakfast." She followed me and I had to keep my hands to myself.

"No Alex. You should've tried last night." She said and started laughing as she stepped out. I smacked her ass when she bent over to put her panties on.

After we got dressed, we drove to the restaurant in different trucks. Most likely MJ molested Morgan the entire ride. I've never seen him this way with any woman. That's how I know she's the perfect one for him. He still hadn't told her what happened with Carlotta. He says he has a feeling she's going to show up. I think that's why he never allows Morgan to go anywhere without him. We got to the restaurant and the waitress sat us down.

"Look Gabby. I'm not going to beat around the bush. My brother loves you, which means you'll eventually have to come around my family again. Try not to let what happened, keep you from becoming a part of the family." Miguel said as he glanced over the menus. Gabby squeezed my hand.

"I know it was a tragic event for you and it will bond you two forever. Take all the time you need to move past it. Just know, that my mom and sister will come find you to apologize." She tensed up.

"Relax. My pops got in their ass over what happened and they're trying to get back on his good side. They'll seek you out but never bring up what you hear went down in our family's past. My mom and sister had no right to lie hands on you regardless of what you said, but you bringing up our family shit should've never came out your mouth either." She nodded.

"Also, my family is powerful like you said, but we're not hateful and we don't go around terrorizing anyone who don't deserve it. Believe it or not, there are many that love us. Unfortunately, these new enemies are coming for us and until we find out who they are, you may hear a lot of bad shit. Don't listen to gossip. If you want to know anything ask my brother. If it's something he can tell you, he will. Don't stress if he doesn't because some things aren't for everyone. You good with that?" Gabby told him yes.

"Good because I'm hungry for food and something else."

"Miguel I swear to God, if you don't stop saying that."

"What Morgan? Shit, you got a nigga strung the fuck out. I don't care who knows I'm in it all the time." Gabby busted out laughing and Morgan put her head down.

"You have to excuse him Gabby. He says anything he wants but he means well."

"Yea I do. I'm glad you gave my brother another chance. He was getting on my nerves sulking over you."

"That's it Miguel. I'm not playing."

"Alright damn. Yo waitress. Can we order or what?" MJ is rude as hell but that's my fucking brother and I had his back, just like he had mine.

We stayed there eating and laughing for almost two hours. MJ kept getting in trouble but it was good to see Gabby laugh. I don't know how I was going to get her to move with me but I needed her around me all the time.

"Why do you have to live so far away?" My mom asked as we stood in the kitchen making dinner. She and I were very close and this is the first time I've been away for a long period of time.

"Ma, you know my man is there and with everything going on he wants me close."

"I know and you know I love MJ, but it's so far." She whined and put the red onions in the salad.

"Melina, stop bothering her about living over there. It's not like you don't speak everyday and she comes to visit every two weeks."

"Be quiet Bruno damn. I was wearing her down." I busted out laughing when I felt some hands around my waist.

"She's wearing you down baby? You not coming home with me." He kissed the side of my neck.

"What if I said no?"

"What if I throw your ass over my shoulder and take you anyway?"

"But I'm pregnant. You can't do that."

"I'll carry you out of her then. Do I need to show you?"

"HELL NO!" My dad shouted.

"You will not drop my grand baby."

"Dad what about me?"

"What about you? We have to make sure the baby is good. You'll be alright." Miguel started laughing.

"Remember when you want some pussy and I say no because you thought my dad was funny." I whispered in his ear.

"Remember when this dick got you screaming and ready to cum and I pull out." I smacked him on the arm and pushed him out the kitchen.

"It's all good. Me and your pops going out back to play basketball." He pecked my lips and went behind my dad.

It took us another hour to finish dinner and get the table set. My two brothers and sister came down to eat. Eddie is the son my dad had from his ex before he met my mom and BJ is the son he had when he cheated on my mom.

Both of them treated my mom as their own and no one

could tell them different. My sister Anna is my moms surprise baby. She didn't want anymore kids but my dad wasn't having it. After my sister, she ended up needing to have a partial hysterectomy because of the fibroid tumors. Therefore, making it harder to conceive.

All my family loved MJ; especially my brothers. They'd ask him all types of questions about his family life. I swear they thought he was *The Godfather* or some shit. My dad thought it was funny while my mom hated them asking. My brothers were good guys; both in college and Eddie had an job at ESPN when he graduated. She didn't want them to change their lifestyles so I think that's why she'd get mad if they asked questions. She probably assumed they would want to get in the business.

Me and my sister helped my mom clean the kitchen while the guys sat in the living room talking smack over a basketball game. I leaned against the wall staring at my man and couldn't help but wonder what he's hiding. I'm not saying he's cheating on me but there's something. He looked over at me and blew a kiss but Eddie made fun of him and they started play fighting. God placed him back in my life for a reason. I hope it's too live happily ever after.

****

"Are you excited?" I saw Miguel's facial expression change when the doctor told us we were having a girl. We stayed in Jersey for a week because Alex didn't want to go home and Miguel refused to leave him.

"No."

"No." I told him to pull the car over.

"I don't mean it like that Morgan. I'm saying, having a daughter is going to make me kill every newborn boy in the nursery the same day she's born and after. That way, I won't have to kill them later." I busted out laughing.

"Awwwww baby. She's not even here yet and you're already protecting her from heartbreak. Don't worry daddy, Mami will keep you occupied."

"What I tell you about talking like that?" He smirked. Miguel loved the way I spoke Spanish to him. I had no Spanish blood in me but I was very fluent in it. He smiled when he felt my hands on his jeans.

122

"I don't remember what you said. But I do know this needs to be handled." I told him. He was brick hard and rubbing my hair as I placed my mouth on him.

"Damn Morgan. You do papi real good."

"Mmmmm. I want that dick to cum in my mouth." He loved when I talked dirty. He pulled over on the side of the rode.

"Shittttttt. Oh shit baby. Fuckkkkkk."

"I went crazy on his dick and he erupted in my mouth. I didn't stop sucking until I knew he was drained. His breathing slowed down and he stared at me.

"I love the hell out of you." He grabbed my face and stuck his tongue in my mouth. I wanted to climb on top of him but being five and half months with this stomach, I couldn't.

"I love you too. Now get me home so I can feel you." He smiled and got us home quick. We stayed in bed the rest of the day. He catered to me all night and I fell asleep with my head on his chest. Being with him isn't as bad as I thought it would be.

****

123

I tried to get out the bed but his arms were on me tight. I moved around a little and finally pushed them off to go to the bathroom. I started the shower and got myself ready for the day. I made breakfast for him and sat in the office to start my schoolwork.

I transferred to online classes to finish school faster. My degree is in communications but I'm getting my Masters in Social Work. I wanted to open my own home for teenage runaways. It would give them the opportunity to not only be successful in the work force but growing up in today's society.

I heard Miguel yelling on the phone and went upstairs to check on him. He was sitting on the bed with a stressed look on his face. He didn't know I was there and I didn't make myself known. The feelings I had were still there about him cheating and I wanted to know if he were.

"I would never fuck with you again. My woman is more than enough." I heard him say. Now who in the hell would he be speaking to like that?

"If you ever go near her, I will kill you."

"You heard what the fuck I said. My woman is off

limits. This shit is between you and me." The person must've been talking shit on the phone.

"Like I said. I don't want you."

"Miguel is everything ok?" He looked up and disconnected the call.

"I'm good Morgan. It's work shit." He moved past me and hopped in the shower. I noticed he took the phone with him, which is something he never does. Now I could be over reacting but it sounds like he's cheating but then again he told the person he didn't want them. I sat on the bed and waited for him to come out.

"Who is she?" He jumped when I spoke.

"Who is who?" His phone started to ring.

"Her." I pointed to the dresser where he put it.

"There is no her Morgan. I would never cheat on you. Don't over think shit because it's going to drive you crazy."

"Ok soooooo, I hear my man up here going off. I come in and he hangs the phone up. Now his phone is ringing off the hook. You tell me what I'm supposed to think." I stood there waiting for an answer.

"I'm not about to pacify you about shit you cooked up in your head." I snatched his phone off the dresser and he grabbed my arm.

"I told you there is no one else. The minute you feel like you don't trust me; the door is right there." He used his eyes to point in the direction of the door.

"Oh it's that easy huh?"

"Not right now Morgan. I have to get to work and.-"

"And my ass nigga. You've been on some sneaky shit lately and if I noticed it, then so has everyone else. I don't know why, but I feel like I'm the only one who doesn't know what's going on. You expect me to sit around and wait for you to come home everyday because you're scared for me to leave the estate. Is she why? What, you don't want me to run into you parading her around?" He laughed and walked out.

"If you leave this house without telling me something, I can guarantee, I won't be here when you return." He stopped and turned around.

"Your threats don't scare me Morgan." He began walking up the steps to where I was.

126

"If you want to go, then go, but if anything happens to my daughter, you'll see a side of me, you've never seen. Fuck with it if you want." I started to go behind him and talk shit but that's how women get fucked up. They keep going; he gets pissed off and snaps. No thanks. I'm good over here. I let him walk right out the door. I sat in the bed for an hour trying to calm down. My baby was doing flips in my stomach and there was a lot of pressure.

Once I felt better, I got up, pulled a few bags out and began putting the things I bought in them. He knew I wasn't here for his money but I still won't take shit he brought me. I left the Rolex, the diamonds, shoes, purses and the other shit.

One thing my mama taught me was, if you feel like he's cheating; he is. And if he's not, there's something he doesn't want you to know about a woman he's dealt with. If that's the case, whatever it is, he believes it will destroy your relationship and do anything to keep it hidden. In my opinion Miguel was definitely doing something he had no business.

My mom went through a lot with my dad and she always told me his love outweighed her thoughts of leaving. I loved Miguel with all my heart but I can't live with a man who's full of secrets.

I know leaving is hard because someone is watching the estate but my plan is to leave when it gets dark. He doesn't usually get in until after seven anyway.

"Mommy can you buy me a plane ticket?" I asked my mom when she picked the phone up.

"What time are you looking to leave?" She never asked questions until I was in front of her.

"Now if I could, but I'm going to wait. At least until it's dark out. That way security will assume everyone is in for the night."

"Honey there's one leaving in two hours."

"Fine. I'm on it." I hung up and got in the car. I told security I needed to go shopping and as usual they blew their breath out. They hated for me to make them come. I had the plan in my head. I would drive one of the cars and have them follow me. I'll purchase an outfit, pretend to use the bathroom and sneak out. It was perfect and I was going to execute it well.

"Hello Morgan." I turned around and saw some Spanish chick smirking at me. She was very pretty and had a banging body.

"Do I know you?"

"No, but I know your man." I sucked my teeth.

"Everyone knows my man." She laughed like what I said was the biggest joke ever.

"No sweetie. I really know your man." She moved in front of me.

"What do you want?"

"I just want you to know that your man isn't as faithful as you think." I wonder if this is who he spoke to this morning.

"Let me guess. You fucked him."

"Yes and it was really good."

"Yea ok." I started to leave.

"Does he lift one of your legs up and let the other one hang off the bed as he slides his big ass dick inside." She put her index finger in her mouth as if she were getting turned on thinking about it.

129

I turned around and moved closer to her. She was loud as hell and I didn't want my security to think something was wrong. I wanted to hear what she had to say. Maybe it will make me leaving him, the right thing to do.

"What he and I do is none of your business."

"Does he smack you on the ass and tell you to cum." I was becoming more and more angry because these are some of the things he and I did.

"Shit, I can barely fit his dick in my mouth but it doesn't stop him from letting me suck it. You wanna see." I tried to move but she put the phone in my face. Sure enough Miguel was sitting on a couch getting head from her. She fast-forwarded a bit and after he came, she jumped on top and rode him. He didn't look to be upset or anything. I saw the date at the top of the phone and became infuriated because we were together at the time.

"Ok, so you have proof you fucked him. And." I continued walking.

"I'm going to keep on sleeping with him too. Girl, you can't handle all of him so I'm just going to borrow him two or three times a week." She was hysterical laughing.

"If you can get it that much, then he isn't my man, now is he? I suggest you find someone else to bother because you showing me a video, won't make me leave him."

"Dumb bitch just like the rest of them."

"Yup. I'll be that." I waved my hand as I walked away. If I weren't pregnant, I'd mop the floor with her ass. I went in the bathroom, changed clothes and hauled ass out of there. I wanted to cry but I'd lose control of the car being blinded by tears, so I held them in.

I hopped out the car and left it running with all my belongings except my purse. I'm sure when they find out whose car it is, they'll contact him but I'll be long gone. I sent him a text before going inside.

Me: *You said you would never cheat on me but I saw a video of you allowing a woman to touch you. She gave you pleasure that only I was supposed to. I'm not going to ask how could you because then I'd be playing the dumb girlfriend. I knew something was up and you left me looking like a fool. When I have the baby, I'll contact you. Stay the fuck away from* *me.* I hit send and waited to see if he read it. Once I saw he did, my phone rang. I shut it off, tossed it in the trash walked in the airport. He can keep those problems.

Good riddance Miguel!

MJ

I read the message Morgan sent me and flew out my office. I called her back to back but she shut the phone off. I had to get home before she really left me. I told her she could but I was mad about the phone call. I planned on apologizing later when I got home but it might be too late. I never cheated on Morgan and I didn't plan on it. My phone started ringing and it was her security detail.

"Yo."

"Ummm boss. Morgan is ugh."

"She what nigga? Where is she?" I became aggravated listening to one of her bodyguards stutter.

"That's just it. We don't know."

"Meet me at the gate." If they didn't know where she was, it meant they weren't paying attention. Morgan is smart as hell and if she wanted to disappear she could. I had ways to find her but her pops used to fuck with those who ran the underground. They are people who get lost and wiped off the earth. Meaning, you never know they existed and the crazy part

133

would be, that they were alive. I had a lot of resources and yes I would find her, but it would take time and I didn't have it to waste.

I parked at the gate and the two dudes appeared to be nervous and they should. They explained what happened and I had to smirk. Morgan had to have had the shit planned before she left the house. I let one off in both of their heads, opened the gate and sped to my house. I called Pablo and told him he had two packages here and to let the head of security know, he's down two people.

I ran up the steps and saw everything still in place. I opened the drawers and noticed the only things missing are things I didn't buy. She took whatever she purchased and left everything else. My phone rang again; this time from Elaina telling me the airport called and said my vehicle was being towed. Someone left it running and there were clothes in the trunk.

Damn! She really left me.

I sat on the bed with my head in my hands thinking of all the reasons I should go after her. Unfortunately, this is the second time I ran her away and I doubt she'll want to hear from me. I'll give her a few days with her family before I bring her back.

I drove to my office pissed off at the world and slammed the door when I got there. I didn't want to be home or at my parents. I took multiple shots of Remy and thought about how I would make this up to Morgan. I fell asleep in my chair and dreamed she was home giving me head. It felt real as hell and I came so hard, it woke me up out my sleep.

"Yo what the fuck?" I snapped when I saw Elaina standing over me naked; wiping her mouth. She didn't give me a chance to stand up and put me in her mouth again. The more I pushed her off, the better it felt. I guess me pushing, made her suck harder.

"Get up Elaina." She sat on my lap and rode me pretty good. I can't even lie.

"Bend over." I already fucked up so I may as well finish. I grabbed the condom out my drawer and went to work on her pussy. I took all my anger out on it and had her screaming. By the time we finished, it was damn near midnight.

I handed her clothes to her and went in the bathroom to wash my dick off.

I came out to see Morgan standing there with tears in her eyes. I don't know when she got here or what she saw, but I was fucked. Elaina walked out the bathroom in just her pants and bra so if Morgan didn't know before, she damn sure knew now.

"I see you got what you've been waiting for." She said to Elaina and hock spit in her face. I know Morgan wanted to hit her but she wouldn't because of my daughter in her stomach. I looked at Elaina and dared her to try something.

Morgan walked out after she left an envelope on my desk. I opened it up and there was an ultrasound for a baby and it said, *"Congratulations you'll be a step mommy"*. I ran down stairs to catch her.

"What is this you left on my desk?"

"The envelope was in my purse when I went to grab my ID to get on the plane. The woman must've dropped it in there. I had every intention of leaving you after I saw the video. I got to the airport but I couldn't board the plane. My heart and love

136

for you wouldn't let me get on. I figured you slipped up and we could get through it." She wiped her tears.

"I sat at the airport for hours waiting for you to come get me and now I see why you didn't." I ran my hand over my head a few times before speaking.

"Morgan you were right on my birthday, when you said she wanted me. The flirting continued and it turned me on but I never cheated. I went home to find you and realized you left me. I came to the office, had a few drinks and fell asleep. She woke me up by giving me head. She got me up again and I fucked her. I'm not going to lie and say it was a mistake or make excuses either. I was fully aware of what I was doing. " She rolled her eyes.

"I didn't sleep with her until tonight. I should've stopped it but I let it happen. Do I regret it? Yes. Would I sleep with her again? Probably. I know I lost you for good after this so I'm not going to pretend I'll stay celibate. As far as someone else having my baby, that's bullshit."

"Thanks for being brutally honest. I wish you had done this before I got pregnant. But make no mistake Miguel. I have every intention of returning the favor."

"WHAT?" I ran after her.

"You heard me. Have a good night." She pulled off in the other car from the house. I guess she went home to find me and realized I wasn't there and came here. How could I be so stupid and fall victim to pussy? Morgan warned me about Elaina but I didn't listen. And not only that, I have to find out whose putting a baby on me.

"I'm not going to apologize for you getting caught. Just know whenever you want this, I'm down." She kissed me on the cheek and got in her car. I guess I may as well do the same. I locked up and took my ass to a hotel.

****

It's been three months and Morgan still wasn't fucking with me. I sent flowers, candy, cards, clothes and anything else I could think of. None of it was accepted and what could be returned, was. I went to her parents' house and she refused to come out the room. I stayed there for two days and nothing. I can't say she was being stubborn because she was hurt and I'm the one who did it.

I did sleep with Elaina a few more times in my office but I fired her after the last time. She started becoming possessive and telling people we were together. My mom got wind of it and let my ass have it. Then Joy cursed me out and I deserved it. Morgan is the perfect woman for me and here I messed up.

Today, I'm on my way to the states because her due date is coming and I wanted to be close. My dad was keeping an eye on things for me, which as of right now isn't much. After the shootout and my cousin getting hit, things died down. We know they're lurking and watching us and we're ready to attack when show their faces.

I got in the car waiting for me, and DJ was in there smoking. I told him I would stop by but I guess he had some things he wanted to speak privately about. He passed me the blunt and had the driver roll the partition up.

My phone was going off and it was a text from Morgan saying she was in labor. Thanks goodness I did come early. I told DJ we would talk after the delivery but not to forget. I was never one to let conversations go because they could be important and hold vital information.

"Hey MJ. How did you get here so quick?" Her dad asked when I stepped out the elevator.

"I booked a hotel room so I could be close when she delivered. I didn't know it would be the same day I got here. I'm glad I came though." Her mom stepped out the room to speak and told me to go see her. This is the first time we laid eyes on each other since the break up. I didn't expect her to look beautiful as she did.

"How are you?" I asked and sat on the bed.

"About to deliver our daughter."

"I miss you like crazy Morgan.-" She didn't say anything.

"Why didn't you accept the stuff I sent you?"

"Its going to take much more than shoes and purses to get me back." I smirked because her comment gave me a little hope. I placed my hand on her stomach and answered the face time call from my mom. She had my brother last week and couldn't be here. The two of them spoke for a few minutes when she squeezed my arm. I turned around and the machines started beeping fast.

"What's wrong?" She dropped the phone and I saw pain in her eyes.

"Her water broke Miguel. She's ok." Her mom said and I looked at Morgan who was crying. The doctor came in, checked her and said she was ready to push. Two hours later she gave birth to my daughter Arcelia Rose Rodriquez, weighing seven pounds, nine ounces. Arcelia is Spanish and her name stands for "*Treasure Chest*." She's definitely our treasure.

"We'll be back tomorrow." Her parents said and left. Everyone from my family came to visit and it was like a party in here. It was after nine and everyone had finally gone home.

Morgan was in the bathroom with the nurse washing up and I had my daughter asleep on my chest. I felt a presence at the door and it was Zariah. I don't know how she got up here but I wasn't complaining. She had stress written on her face but overall she looked a lot better.

"She's so pretty MJ. Can I hold her?" Zariah was still moving a little slow but it didn't slow her down. She washed her hands and took a seat. I passed her my daughter and stared at how she held her.

"I would've been a good mommy MJ." I saw her eyes tearing up. I know the shit with Akeem had her going crazy.

"Zariah he knows that."

"Does he? He gave another woman what he promised to only me." I heard the bathroom door open. Morgan smiled when she saw Zariah holding Arcelia. She asked the nurse to close the door and for me to trade spots with her. I moved to the bed and she sat in the chair.

"Zariah, do you still love him?" She nodded her head and wiped the tears falling from her face.

"Then why aren't you with him?"

"I don't know. To be honest, I was with someone else on the break we took."

"Oh hell no." I lifted my daughter up.

"What's wrong MJ?"

"My daughter doesn't need to hear you were a thot. What if she remembers that shit?" They both laughed but I was serious as hell.

"I know it hurt Zariah. Shit, you know what I've gone through with him and unfortunately, he's going to be in my life forever."

"Damn right and I wish you would fuck somebody else." She waved her hand at me.

"I won't but he'll eat my pussy."

"WHAT YOU SAY?" I laid my daughter down and walked on the side of the bed to her.

"Miguel, I'm trying to comfort her and you're making this about you. Go on now." She waved me off.

"Hurry up Zariah because we need to talk."

"Nope. She's staying up here all night." Zariah looked from her to me and kept laughing.

"I got you Morgan. Don't even worry. I got a trick for that ass." I laid in the bed and picked the remote up.

"Anyway, if you did you, then why are you so upset? I mean, yes, he had a baby but you did the same thing."

"I used protection."

"Ok, but we all know stupid niggas don't think quick on their feet like we do." She looked at me.

143

"Keep testing me Morgan. I swear to God." They thought shit was funny.

"Anyway. If you can't get past him having a baby that we all know he doesn't want, then move on. However, if you still want to be with him and the baby won't be an issue, then I say, go get your man back."

"Are you and MJ getting back together?" I waited to hear her answer.

"Nope. This nigga got another woman pregnant and we were a couple. He can be with that bitch." She stood up and got in the bed with me.

"Believe that shit if you want Zariah. Morgan talk big shit but she know what it is." My daughter woke up and was ready to eat. I took her from Morgan after she finished.

"MJ, mommy did say aunt Violet told her.-"

"I don't give a fuck what my mother said. I don't have any other kids." I was getting aggravated now.

"Boy, don't talk to me like that. I'm telling." She picked her phone up and called Heaven. She knows I hate hearing her mothers' mouth.

144

"Miguel Rodriquez, do not make me come up there and smack your ass. Zariah is your cousin and Morgan is your woman."

"Ex woman Heaven." She screamed out and I could've smacked her.

"You treat them with the same respect you want people to treat me and your mom." Zariah stuck her tongue out. I stayed on the phone a little longer and handed the phone to Zariah. I gave Arcelia to Morgan, stood up and opened the door.

"Get out Zariah. You up in here starting shit." She stood up, kissed the baby and Morgan and came towards me.

"I done been kicked out of better hellholes than this." She mushed me in the head and tried to run down the hall. I chased her and something was off.

"Zariah." She turned around.

"GET DOWN!" Gunfire erupted in the hallway. She pulled her piece out and started shooting with me. By the time we finished the nurses were crying, doctors were yelling and two men were on the floor.

145

"PULL THE TRUCK AROUND TO THE FRONT." I yelled in the phone. I walked in the room and Morgan had my daughter with her in the closet. I helped her out and had her get dressed. Once she told me she was fine, I went back in the hallway.

"You good." I asked Zariah who was standing over the men.

"I'm good. How's Morgan?"

"She's good. A little shaken up but good. Who are these motherfuckers?"

"No clue cousin."

"Snap a photo on your phone and send them to me. They're coming after my woman, my daughter and my cousin. Oh yea, its about to be a fucking war."

"ROUND EVERYONE UP! WE'RE ABOUT TO LIGHT THIS FUCKING CITY UP!" I hung the phone up and got my family out of there.

DJ

"DJ I think I'm.-"

"Hold on Savannah." I picked my phone up and it was MJ telling me to round everyone up. I'm not sure what went on but if he said it, it means we're about to make a mess. What I mean by that is, the city is about to bleed. I sent a group text out and got up.

"What were you saying Savannah?" I went in my closet and grabbed anything black I had. I felt her arms on my waist.

"We can talk about it later. Be careful." I turned around and stared in her eyes.

"You sure?" I pecked her lips and she jumped in my arms.

"Am I all you need in a woman?" I laid her on the bed. It seemed like the shit with Akeem having a baby on my sister and MJ cheating on his woman made everyone else's chick feel insecure.

"All that and then some. Don't second guess your spot in my life." She nodded her head and I put the covers on her.

147

"I'm going to lock up. Do not and I repeat Savannah, do not open the door for anyone. My family has the keys here if they want to come. Matter of fact; don't even go to the door. If you hear someone knocking, call me on the phone and I promise to answer."

"Should I just go home?"

"I want you here when I get here but if you're more comfortable there, I won't be upset. I can come to you."

"I'm ok. I'll wait for you here."

"I can't wait for you to get pregnant. You think we'll have twins?" She went to speak but my phone went off again.

"I'll call you in a few." I kissed her, locked up the house and jumped in my car. I drove to the place we held our meetings at and everyone was there; including AJ, who I haven't really spoken to unless it dealt with business. Neither of us said one word to the other and walked in.

"First off. DJ, get the shit off your chest with AJ now. I'm not about to have us go to war and you got a chip on your shoulder."

"I'm good MJ." AJ told him.

148

"Fuck it. You knew that nigga cheated on my sister and you smiled in my face. I know it's a bro code but that's my sister and you were considered a brother to us."

"Nigga my entire family found out when y'all did. I approached him in the hospital because I thought he caused Zariah to get shot. I was ready to rock his ass. So before you think I shitted on her, you should've asked. You're mad at me over that but did you tell your cousin about the pregnant bitch over here looking for him? Talking about I'm keeping secrets. That bitch been here two weeks and by the look on his face I can tell you didn't."

"What the fuck is he talking about DJ? Don't tell me you holding out."

"This ain't over AJ."

"Yes the fuck it is. He told you he didn't know and was ready to rock his own blood over Zariah. Get over the shit." I looked at my sister and she nodded her head. Akeem had his head down the entire time. We didn't hang with him much but if we had beef he was always down. He isn't into the streets like us but he wasn't a punk either. I know he loved my sister,

149

hell we all did, but he fucked up.

"Now what's this about some bitch?"

"I don't know who she is. I was going to tell you in the truck but Morgan went into labor. Whoever she is, she found me at mall and picked me out of everyone there, which let me know she's aware of me being your cousin. She went on and on about some foul shit she did to you." I saw his facial expression change. He had no reaction and I wasn't going to repeat what she said. It's obvious no one knew.

"What did she do?" Zariah asked and MJ told her nothing. I don't know why he hid it.

"Anyway, she claims you're her baby daddy and she wanted you to be present when she delivered."

"We have eyes on the people who sent those niggas to the hospital." He didn't acknowledge what I said about the chick and had us getting ready for war. Its crazy how I just mentioned some chick claiming him to be her baby daddy and he sparked up a new conversation.

James Jr. came in saying he had a truckload of guns and Darius was pulling the ammunition out his duffle bags. They never liked to travel with them together. They said if by some chance they got caught at least they wouldn't have loaded guns. Not that it mattered with the amount of shit they had, but hey, that's their shit.

"Who is this PJ nigga?"

"That's Tara's brother." Akeem said.

"Who the fuck is Tara?"

"His baby mama." Zariah stood up and left the room.

"My had Akeem. I didn't know."

"It's all good MJ. That's her brother and to my knowledge a petty hustla. I don't know a lot because I haven't spoken to her but word on the street is, he's in deep with some foreigners. They put him on their team to get at us. I found that out through my pops and uncle. They had beef with some Africans, who come to find out, is my grandfather. He's been investigating to find out if they're behind all the shit. Somehow they're connected to your pops as well."

"Yea, he exterminated some Africans for disrespecting my mom and putting a hit on her. If it is connected, then all of us are sitting ducks because we don't know who they are.

151

Luckily, I have eyes on their so called workers but whoever the woman behind the scene running it all, is like a ghost."

"So this goes back to our parents enemies." I asked remembering MJ mentioning it before he took over.

"Exactly. However, Ahmad had a son who we have eyes on. He doesn't do much but work and go home to his family. I could kill him but he may come in handy so I'm allowing him to breathe a little longer. Your grandfather had two sons besides your pops in case you didn't know. I haven't heard if the other son had kids but his daughter did."

"Yea, but my aunt had her put in a human trafficking ring and no one has seen her. If it is her kid, then we have to find him."

"That's right. My mom did say they tried to sell her but my dad found her and they did it to them instead. I didn't know she had kids." AJ said.

"Mannnnn, ain't nobody from Africa over here. You keep listening.-"

"DJ! OUTSIDE NOW!" MJ yelled and everyone looked at me. I stood up and shut the door after I stepped out. We were in the lounge area.

"Yo. You're my cousin and I love you but you're about to make me fuck you up."

"Whatever." I waved him off. He grabbed my arm, twisted it up my back and slammed my face on the wall.

"You know I don't tolerate disrespect and you being my blood, doesn't excuse you. I called you out here because you're making a fool of yourself over shit that has nothing to do with you. I understand she's your sister but leave that shit alone."

"Fuck you MJ!" I was fuming that he had me against the wall.

"Fuck me nigga." He let me go.

PHEW! He shot me in the arm and instantly, I felt the blood gushing out.

"This is my last time telling you DJ. Get out that funk you're in and get your head in the game. You're mad at the wrong person."

"You really shot me." He stood there staring at me.

"The next one you won't survive." He shoulder checked me and opened the door.

"Zariah go get the bullet out your brothers arm." I heard him say when he walked out.

"Yo, for real MJ." I heard AJ say and he came in here. I slid down the wall in pain. The shit was burning like a motherfucker.

"What the fuck DJ? You know your cousin don't play when it comes to business." AJ was helping Zariah open up gauze pads. I could hear MJ still talking as if nothing happened. They helped me on the table and my sister used something to remove the bullet and I screamed out. She stitched me up and placed some bandages on it.

"DJ, I'm not angry about you taking up for me. But you can't take it out in everyone. We are family whether it's through blood or not and what your doing is breaking us up and for what? He had a baby, but we weren't together. If I want to be upset, that's up to me, not you." She kissed my cheek and started cleaning up.

"My bad AJ."

"It's all good. I probably would've reacted the same way but I never would've come for MJ. What the fuck were you

154

thinking?"

"He bleeds just like we do."

"He does but you know he takes no prisoners. Family or not, disrespect is disrespect and you would've handled the situation the same way. You're lucky he didn't kill you."

"I will the next time." MJ came in with everyone else following.

"There won't be a next time cuz. I should've never.-"

"It's water under the bridge. But after all that, who came in here?" I remained silent.

"Exactly. AJ is your brother nigga and you treated him like shit and he still had your back. We all we got." He said as everyone else agreed.

"If motherfuckers see us beefing, it becomes easy for them to get us. If they see how strong we are, there's no way for them to catch us slipping. A solid foundation can never be broken when you have a strong team."

"And that's exactly why you're in charge. You be saying some deep shit." James Jr. said.

"You good." MJ asked before he started speaking.

"I'm good."

"These are the spots were hitting tonight. I want them all hit at the exact same time. This will let them know we're onto them and it won't allow them time to call and warn anyone. When we're done, I want everyone to head home, and send a message that their crew is accounted for and the job was complete. Are there any questions?" No one said a word as we all headed out. Zariah got in the car with us and we pulled off.

By the time we finished, eight trap houses were burned down, families affiliated with anyone working the trap houses or the ones who shot at them in the hospital, were exterminated. The captain of the police department called MJ and asked if he could go back to P.R. I guess he knew from the damage it was him. We all got a kick out of that.

I went home and snuck in the bed behind Savannah. I laid my arm across her stomach and closed my eyes. Tonight, my cousin put a lot of shit in perspective and instead of moving on from what happened to Zariah, I was stuck defending her over a choice her ex made. I don't regret it because she's still my sister but I understand.

156

"I'm pregnant." She whispered and backed up closer to me.

"Thanks baby for giving me what I wanted." I kissed the back of her neck and went to sleep with a smile on my face.

****

"What the fuck were you thinking?" My dad was going in on me about the shit with my cousin. Zariah told him what happened and I've been here all day listening to him and my mom curse me out.

"Listen son. They may be your relatives but those in the Rodriquez family are nothing to fuck with. MJ is worse than his father; hell even big Miguel told us that. You're lucky all he did is shoot you in the arm. He could've killed you."

"I know and we peaced it up. It won't happen again."

"It better not." My dad walked off and my mom sat next to me.

"I know it's a little nerve wrecking to have your cousin come over and steal the spotlight." I gave her the side eye.

"You, AJ and Alex Jr. run things over here but when he

comes everyone looks to him. Son, you know it has nothing to do with not respecting you, but remember he is the one who supplies you. If he cuts you off then what? I know you have money but I also know you like the power you possess. Who wouldn't? I don't want you getting into with him. I will definitely fuck him up if he killed you, but would it be justified when you're the one who disrespected him first?"

"Ma."

"It's ok to have those feelings. But I'm sure your cousin doesn't even look at it the way you do. He's used to being in charge and honestly, he's good at it from what I hear. He's smart DJ and calculates his moves before jumping in headfirst. Don't bite the hand that feeds you. I love you." She kissed my forehead and got up.

I sat there thinking about everything my mom said and she's right. I am used to running shit but when he comes, people look to him. I'm not jealous but I do feel some type of way. I would never step on his toes when he's in charge but I know not to ever come for him again either. I don't know why he got so angry, when I wave him off, all the time. I guess it's

158

true when they say; it's a time and place for everything.

"Oh ma. Savannah is pregnant." I said walking out the door and saw a look of sadness in Zariah's face.

"I didn't know you were here sis. I'm sorry."

"Don't be. I'm fine. Everyone thinks I'm going to spaz out again but I'm not. Do you think she'll have twins?"

"I hope so. I only want two kids."

"Boy be quiet. You're ready to marry that girl so it won't matter how many she has."

"Whatever. I'll see you later." I mushed her and walked out the door.

Zariah

I couldn't believe someone tried to come for us at the hospital. What made matters worse, was my brother being in his feelings over the shit with Akeem. Yes, I'm hurt but what can I do? It was during a break that I wanted because he wouldn't give me a baby.

Now his son is going on four months and from what his sister tells me, he won't have anything to do with him. She told me he sends her money once a month and that's it. Her mom gets him but she always tells him when he's coming, and he leaves.

Today, I was on a mission and some may call me crazy but sometimes we do crazy things for people we love. I pulled up in front of the house and noticed a few dudes sitting on the porch. I made sure my nine was in my back and my .22 was in my sock. I hit the alarm on my car and walked over to the gate. The guys stared at me with lust in their eyes. I went to knock and it was opened.

I saw a woman laid out on the couch watching

television. She didn't even acknowledge me come in and told me to move out the way. How the hell you don't speak but tell someone to move? I made my way to where I heard a woman talking and there she was sitting with some ratchet ass bitches.

"Can I speak to you for a minute?"

"Well, if it isn't the stuck up bitch trying to be a doctor. What can I do for you?" She put her phone down and pulled the gum out her mouth on her finger and started playing with it. What in the hell was he thinking fucking her?

"Privately." One of the girls sucked her teeth. I grabbed her hair and banged her face on the table. I could hear her nose crack.

"Bitch." The other chick stood up and I kicked her so hard in the chest she flew against the back door and hit her head on the dead bolt, knocking her dumb ass out. Another chick came out the bathroom, looked at them, then me and stepped out the kitchen. *Punk ass.*

"Now that I have your undivided attention. I came to pick up your son Jacob."

"For what? His father doesn't even see him so why are

you here?"

"Tara, I will beat the brakes off you, wait for you to recover and do it again. Don't question me about shit. Go get him."

"Hold up. Is that Zariah?" I heard behind me.

"Go get him now bitch." She got up slow and put her hands up in surrender. I pulled my nine out and had it on his forehead.

"Who the fuck are you and how do you know my name?"

"I'm PJ. The one who used to go with Gabby. Yo, you wild as hell. You did this?" He pointed to the chicks in the kitchen.

"Yup. Now if you'll excuse me." I saw Tara coming down the steps and couldn't help but smell shit.

"Bitch, if you don't take him upstairs and change him, I swear we're going to have a problem." She had the nerve to roll her eyes.

"Who the hell are you?" The woman on the couch must've finally realized I was there.

"Nobody." I stood there waiting and felt like she was taking too long and went up the steps.

"I don't know how much longer she's going to wait. You need to get here fast."

"I'm ready." I kicked the door open and noticed how filthy the room was.

"I should report your dirty ass to child services. How the hell are you allowing him to live in this filth? Akeem gives you a decent amount of money each month. You know what? Who cares? We out!" I didn't want to touch the car seat because it too was filthy but he was a baby and I had to get him out of there. I strapped him in and felt some one behind me.

"Can I help you nigga?"

"You sexy as hell." He was cute when he licked his lips but I don't know if he was trying to keep me there or if he was for real. After the phone call I heard Tara on, it's best to leave and that's exactly what I did.

My first stop was babies r us where I picked him up a new car seat, stroller, some lotion, baby wash, diapers and cute outfits. I wanted to go to the mall but ugh he needed a bath. I stopped at the food store to pick up some things for my house and got him a few cans of milk and some of those baby snacks.

I pulled up in my driveway, took him out, put him in the house and removed everything else from my truck. I sent his father a message and asked him to stop by so we could talk. I know he would be shocked because we haven't spoken since I found out.

I gave Jacob a bath and I was disgusted by the amount of dirt that came off. Akeem's mom told me she hated to drop him off because Tara wasn't taking care of him good, but I thought she was saying it to make me feel less upset about it.

I washed him in the lavender body wash and used the lotion on his dry skin. I fed him a jar of baby food, gave him bottle and laid in the bed with him. I got a text from his father that he was outside.

"Hey." I let him step in and closed the door.

"You ok?" He stared at me.

"I'm fine Akeem." I pointed to the couch for him to sit.

"I miss you Zariah." Once he said that, I leaned in to kiss him and he backed up.

"Zariah I can't."

"Why not?"

"Because I'm going to want more." He said. I stood up and took my shirt off, along with my bra and the rest of my clothes. I straddled his lap and we began kissing each other feverishly. We were like animals in heat.

"Damn, I missed talking to my best friend." He slid his tongue up and down my pussy and I came right away. It's been months since we've been together and I couldn't hold out. He put two fingers in and brought two more out. I tried to keep my moans low but it was hard.

"Shit, I miss you so much Zariah. I want you back." I saw him letting his tears fall as he made love to me. This is the second time he cried over me.

"I'm scared Akeem and.-" I now had my own tears falling.

"I don't want us to ever break up again if you take me back." I felt him stop and slide something on my finger as he laid on top of me. I pushed him off me and sat up crying. I looked up at him.

"I wanted to propose the night you got shot. I had everything waiting for you at the house. I don't want anyone else. Please say you'll marry me."

"Yes baby. Yes." I cried some more. He laid me back down and made love to me until I couldn't take anymore. He came in me each time and I prayed he got he pregnant.

"Come take a shower." He lifted me up and walked in the bathroom in my room. I don't think he paid any attention to his son lying there.

"I want you to have my kids. I was holding out so you didn't have any distractions. I never wanted you to regret not finishing school because of a baby. I'm sorry for not strapping up and.-" he had his forehead on mine. I knew he was sorry and we weren't together so I couldn't really be mad.

"Let me cum in you again tonight."

"Akeem, I don't think. Shitttttt." He rammed himself in me and we had rough sex in the shower and a bitch loved it.

"Akeem, I need to tell you something." I said as he dried me off.

"Yea baby."

"Promise you won't get mad." Just as I was about to speak, Jacob started crying. He stopped and looked at me. I ran in the room with my robe and picked him up.

"Whose kid is that?" I thought he was joking but the look on his face told me he was serious. I couldn't believe he had no clue what his son looked like but then again, he never stayed at his mom's long enough to see his face.

"Akeem meet Jacob. Jacob this is your dad."

"I'm out." I laid the baby in the car seat and went downstairs.

"Akeem stop it. Stop this shit right now."

"Zariah, I don't want that kid."

"Akeem look at me." I turned his face to me.

"I should be the one running away but I'm not. I went to get him and brought him here to show you I was ok. What I'm not ok with, is how you're taking out on him what you did."

"His mother isn't you."

"So what. You made a mistake and we have to deal with it. He's going to be my stepson and I'll be damned if you're a deadbeat." He fell on the couch and put his head in his hands.

"Akeem he's here now. I love you and we'll get through this. If you can't be around your son, then I won't marry you." He popped his head up

"How the hell did I mess up with you?" He pulled my face close to his and kissed me with so much passion, had the baby not started crying, we'd be having more make up sex. I went to get him and brought him downstairs. I changed him and fixed a bottle.

"I don't know how to hold a baby Zariah. You do it." He pushed him away.

"You need to get practice for when our baby comes." He smiled and took Jacob from me.

"You better not be on birth control."

"I'm not and ugh… When he goes back to sleep, I got a surprise for you." I blew him a kiss and decorated my bedroom with the sex toys I got from the store last week. I thought I'd introduce him to the baby first but it never works out the way you want.

"He's asleep." I closed the door so he couldn't look

inside and we put Jacob in the guest bedroom. We put a bunch of pillows around him and left the door open. I opened my bedroom door and he got a wicked smile on his face.

"Oh you're definitely getting pregnant tonight."

"I hope so. Come to me daddy."

"Fuck Zariah. You sexy as hell and you know I like when you talk like that." Needless to say my new fiancé and I did a lot of freaky shit.

****

"Bitch you engaged." Morgan shouted when I stopped by to see the baby. MJ popped up off the couch and sucked his teeth.

"Punk ass nigga." Morgan shut the door and went to get the baby.

"Why my man gotta be all that?"

"Because now she's going to want a ring. Fucking bullshit."

"But y'all not together."

"Don't get fucked up. You know she ain't going nowhere."

169

"Whatever Miguel. Here she is Zariah."

"Don't be speaking in thot language in front of her either." I took the baby and sat down next to him.

"I'm happy for you Z. I know how much you two love each other. I can't wait until my new man proposes."

"See this shit is about to get her killed." Morgan waved him off but MJ was dead serious.

"MJ go find your bitch. I'm sure she had the baby by now. Over here driving me crazy." MJ hopped up off the couch and snatched her up.

"Get your ho ass hands off me." She was punching him but he took her upstairs and slammed the door. I've never seen MJ allow anyone besides family to touch him and Morgan was fucking him up, well not bad but in general.

I had Le Le in my arms and couldn't help but to think about how my baby would look. That was the nickname Morgan's mom gave Arcelia. She was so tiny and I loved the way she smelled. I'm not pregnant yet, but a bitch can wonder. I stood up and put her in the swing because I heard some arguing upstairs and then stomping down the steps.

"Fuck you MJ. I'm over this shit." I was confused as to what just happened. He came over to where I was, kissed the baby and was on his way out the door but stopped and stared at Morgan, who was now on the steps hysterical crying. He went over to her and she told him to leave.

"Zariah take care of her." His eyes were glassy.

"What happened?" My ass was confused as hell.

"My phone went off and she looked at it. I don't mind her going through my phone now that we're on better terms."

"Ok, so what happened?"

"It was a message from an unknown number. There was a photo of a kid and.-" He ran his hand down his face.

"What?"

"She looks just like Le Le."

"Oh shit! What are you going to do?"

"I don't know. Tell Morgan I love her more than life itself and is not what she thinks." He gave me a hug and I swore, I saw a tear roll down his cheek. He closed the door and I went upstairs to check on her.

"Zariah can you take Le Le to your mom. I can't deal

right now." I sat by her and relayed the message MJ asked.

"I didn't want to believe it. I never saw the baby and yea I talked shit about it, but it wasn't real until I saw the photo. They could be twins Zariah. Why would he do me like that? And before you say it's the same, it is but it's not. We were together. I thought he was happy but he couldn't have been."

"It's definitely not the same and I understand how hurt you are. Miguel loves you Morgan and you know he's not going to claim the kid until he's a hundred percent sure. Even if the baby is his, he's not going to let you leave him."

"Thanks Zariah. I just need to lie down. My head is hurting really bad." I passed her some aspirin out the bathroom with a cup of water and got Le Le's things ready to go. I'll come check on her later but right now she needs a moment.

Joy

"Whose is it?" My mom asked as I was bent over the toilet puking my guts out.

"I'm sorry mommy."

"Joy, you are a grown woman. Why are you apologizing for it? I mean none of us knew you had a boyfriend but then again, you've been MIA lately."

"It's AJ's." I rested my head on the bathroom wall.

"Does he know?"

"I'm scared he'll ask me to terminate it because he's scared of daddy. Oh my God, daddy's going to be so disappointed in me."

"Relax Joy. Break it to him easy but you know he's going to want AJ to marry you. He's not with you having a baby out of wedlock and then you have kids with someone else and so forth."

"I'm not ready for marriage, hell, I'm barely ready for this kid."

"Looks like you need to invite him here and tell them together. At least you'll get it out the way." I nodded my head, picked myself up off the floor and called AJ.

"What's up baby? You feel better?" I told him I had a cold for the last two days.

"Yea but I'll feel better if you come take care of me."

"Um, how am I supposed to get on the estate without one of your cousins?" I forgot all about that.

"Oh ask Gabby to come with you. I'm sure Alex won't mind seeing her."

"I'll be there tomorrow." We said our goodbyes and I went in my moms' room and laid down with her and my new baby brother. How the hell is my kids' uncle going to be a year older than him?

"He's coming tomorrow."

"Ok. I'll cook dinner and have Abuela come over. You know he is calm in front of her." My dads' mom is down to earth and he tries to play innocent in front of her. My aunt Hazel said he's always been like that. He tries to make his mom think she's the bad kid and he's not.

****

I called my cousin Ricky up because we hadn't been

around each other in a minute. The last time I saw him was at their wedding. Yea, it's legal over here too. My mom and aunt Hazel were a mess getting him ready. He was gorgeous too in his gown and veil. Ryan was decked out in his white tuxedo. MJ was the best man and my brothers were the groomsmen. They said their own vows and I think all the women in attendance cried. They may have been two guys but their love is the same as anyone else's.

Ricky came over and stayed with me all night. Of course, Ryan stalking ass ended up coming over too after he finished whatever MJ had him doing. My brother came back in rare form last week. He won't tell anyone what's going on, but we do know Morgan had a nervous breakdown over it.

Her mom called and said she had to take her to the hospital because she was crying so much it caused her pressure to go high. She had a hard time breathing and her anxiety was bad. My brother flew back over there and stayed but they said, she refused to speak to him. He came in last night and no one has seen or heard from him.

"You ready." My mom asked when I went to her house

175

for dinner. All day I was running around with her. AJ said they would be here around six and it's five thirty. My dad asked why did she cook a lot and she said no reason. I heard the door open and it was Alex who still to this day doesn't speak to me. I saw Gabby and AJ getting out the truck from the window.

"Hello." I spoke to Gabby and she moved past me and went to Alex.

"Give them time baby." AJ said and gave me a quick hug.

"It's been a few months."

"I know but their loss is forever." I understood but he talks to my mom and she was there too. I told him my dad is here and he backed away.

"Hey AJ. I see you brought your sister. Come on Violet. Shit I'm hungry." My dad said and called everyone down to eat. The tension was thick at the table.

"Daddy, I need to tell you something." My father looked at me and I stared at AJ who was about to have a heart attack.

"Whatever you need to tell me can wait. I'm still

176

waiting on your mother to say something." We all looked at her.

"Gabby, I apologize for what happened to you. It wasn't our intentions to cause problems or make you.-" she waved her hand so my mom didn't have to say it.

"No disrespect Mrs. Rodriquez, but to be honest I don't feel as if you meant it." I could see my mom getting angry.

"I'm not asking you to say it again. The reason I say it, is because had your husband not reminded you; those words would have never left your mouth. I do take responsibility for making you come at me from my harsh words but I never laid a hand on you, nor would I ever. What you and your daughter did to me and my mother that day is unforgivable in my eyes. I'm ok not ever speaking to either of you again. Alex, I love you but this wasn't a good idea." She dropped her fork and stood up with AJ doing the same.

"I'M PREGNANT DADDY AND AJ IS THE FATHER." I blurted out.

"WHAT THE FUCK? IS EVERYBODY HAVING A DAMN BABY? FIRST YOUR BROTHERS, THEN YOUR

MOTHER AND NOW YOU." He must've realized what he said.

"I apologize Gabby and Alex, it slipped out." Neither of them said a word. AJ gave me a crazy look and my dad shook his head.

"Goodbye Alex. AJ can we go please?" Gabby was about to cry and Alex sat and slouched down in the chair, looking at the ceiling. So much for having a nice dinner.

"AJ wait." He helped his sister get in the truck.

"Are you crazy Joy? How could you spring that on me in front of your father? I thought you told him about us and he just didn't want me here. Yo, I love you and I'm happy you're having my kid but I'm not with the secretive shit you got going on. My sister came here expecting to spend time with Alex and she's at a dinner with the woman who punched her in the face and the other one who killed her baby. This is fucked up on all levels Joy. I thought you were better than that."

"AJ, I'm sorry. I was scared to tell him and I apologized to Gabby several times. It doesn't bring the baby back but I had no idea she still hated me. I've seen her at your place a few

178

times."

"She tolerated you Joy on the strength of me. That's my sister and she'll never disrespect you unless you do it to her. Gabby isn't built like you and your mom Joy. This type of shit is too much for her and I feel like shit for bringing her here. I'll talk to you later." He hopped in the truck and left me standing there. I felt someone's hand on my shoulder and looked up to see my dad. I broke down and cried in his arms.

"I'm sorry daddy. I didn't mean to get pregnant. I'm in love with him and he was my first."

"It's alright Joy. I'm not happy but you're grown. I wish you would have waited but I'm not mad."

"He left upset."

"Well, I heard what he said and I agree with him. Poor Gabby felt like she was ambushed and it wasn't fair to her, when she blames you and your mom. Look." He lifted my chin.

"Gabby and her mom are quiet, laid back and pretty much homebodies. I know that from speaking with big Aiden."

"When did you talk to him?"

"I called over there not too long ago to apologize for the way you two acted."

"You never apologize."

"You're right but the two of you were wrong and it never should've happened. Joy, they're not into the life we have, so when you and your mom went over there and started fighting them it wasn't anything they're used to."

"But she was talking shit."

"No she wasn't. You're mom told me what she said and it sounded as if she wasn't about to let you or Violet speak to her anyway you wanted. She didn't have to bring up our past but neither of you had a right to hit them."

"If I could take it back I would. Alex hates me and now AJ probably won't speak to me until the baby comes. You and mommy are the only ones who talk to me."

"Right now you can't focus on who speaks to you. The baby is all you should think about now."

"Maybe I should beat it out of you when you turn three months. At least we'll be even and then, I may stop hating you." Alex said and walked off.

"That motherfucker is crazy. What type of kids did we raise?" My dad laughed and told me to stay away from him.

"I want you to stay here a few days. Let me give him time to cool off and then I'll talk to him. I know we think he should be over it now and I believe he is, but when Gabby gets upset over it, he does as well. If you want to get back on his good side, Gabby is the way to go."

"I tried daddy. I've seen her at AJ's and she won't speak but she's not petty either. I don't know what else to do."

"Well. I suggest you think of something if you don't want your brother to kill you." He thought the shit was funny.

"Daddy."

"I'm just playing. I'll talk to him. In the meantime, go help your mother clean up. I need to handle her later."

"Bye daddy."

"What? Your mom has some powerful.-" I covered my ears and walked in the house. My grandmother and Abuela were going in on my mom. When they saw me, it was my turn. At least the hard part is over.

Alex

I had no idea Gabby was coming to visit. When I got to my parents house and she came in, I'm not going to front, I was happy as hell. She looked beautiful in her maxi skirt and fitted shirt. Her sandals tied around her legs and her feet and nails were perfect. She smelled like fruit and I wanted to take her home and away from the disaster I knew was about to happen. I hate that we stayed for the dinner but I love the way she stands up to my mom without being disrespectful. I think my father did too but he'll never say it.

I jumped in my car when they left, picked her up from the airport and brought her back to my house. I wasn't about to let her make the trip for nothing. AJ didn't seem fond of staying so we waited for him to get on the plane. My sister was doing too much and it kept backfiring on her. I guess she realized my parents couldn't fix the shit with her and Gabby. My mom on the other hand could care less about speaking to her and it bothers me, because they started it.

"You better hope I let you go, now that I have you here." She smiled and held my hand as we drove to my house.

"Can we stop to get something to eat? I want to try Spanish food from here."

"What you mean?"

"You know people make Spanish food in the U.S. but it's different when you go to the place it's originated from."

"I'm about to take you someplace where they make the best Spanish food ever." We drove for about twenty minutes and pulled in.

"Ola! Como Esta!" She gave me a hug and kissed my cheek. She pulled Gabby in and did the same thing but held her hand on the way in.

"Gabby you weren't properly introduced. This is my Abuela." We walked in and followed her in the kitchen.

"I know we ate at ma's earlier but she wants to try real Spanish food from here."

"Your mom made.-"

"Exactly. Ma cooks soul food more than anything."

"I'll cook up something."

183

"How are you Gabby?" She looked over at me and I shrugged my shoulders.

"I'm good." Abuela turned around and asked her again but this time told her to be honest.

"Can I speak freely?" We both shook our heads.

"I can't stand your mom and sister. I don't ever want to be around them again. There I said it." Both of us smirked. I guess she thought we'd be mad.

"Why are you smirking?"

"Honey you're not the first or last woman who doesn't like them. Those two are evil if you ask me but I will say, they won't let anything happen to you, even though you feel that way."

"Huh?"

"Violet and Joy mean well, which is why they came to ask about the baby. They didn't want to be a part of what you and Alex went through. However, you showed no fear and they didn't expect it. No one has ever spoken to them the way you have. Honestly, Violet respects you more for standing up to her. She'll never tell you but she does."

"I would never disrespect my elders but.-"

"You don't have to explain anything Gabby. We know and so does she. Do you think you would've been allowed to step foot in her home or on the estate if she didn't like you? Violet is very protective of her children and she knows how much Alex loves you and would rather be in his life, then out of it." I squeezed her leg under the table.

"Now let's get down to the real issue." Abuela put the knife down. She was cutting up peppers and onions. She wiped her hands on the apron and sat down across from her; taking her hand.

"Gabby, what happened to you, happens to a lot of women everyday." Gabby gave her a look.

"It may not go down the same way but women have miscarriages all the time. It's unfortunate how yours came about but honey, you can't be angry forever. I'm not telling you to ever forget what went down but you need to forgive her. I'm not saying it because she's my granddaughter but because the hate is consuming you." Gabby put her head down.

"I know it hurt but this anger is holding you back from

moving ahead with your life. You two love one another but you don't want to be around him here. It's not fair to him and he'll do anything to make you happy. I'm not saying you have to speak to them or even go and accept their apology. You do have to forgive them and live your life the way you were before it happened." Her head was on my shoulder and she had tears coming down her face.

"I'm so angry though."

"And it's ok Gabby but it's been a few months now. If you continue to carry this anger, it will destroy you and any relationship you seek. Listen, why don't you two go away for a few days and get reacquainted."

"Abuela did you just tell us to have sex?"

"I'm no fool and I may be older but you did make a baby. Shit, I want you to get her pregnant again. I want to see some great grandkids before I die. Morgan is the only one and now the shit with the bitch who did the unthinkable to your brother. I may have another one who we won't ever meet, because she's hiding."

"MJ has another baby?" Gabby said and covered her

mouth.

"It's supposed to be his but she won't come around to take a test."

"I know Morgan is upset."

"Yea she is, but it didn't happen the way she thinks and you're probably thinking. It's my brothers story to tell, so don't ask." She nodded and continued talking to my Abuela. By the time they finished, there was a table of food and Gabby had shed more tears. We ate and it was like my abuela had her feeling a lot better.

They exchanged phone numbers and hugged before we left. I got to my house around one in the morning and didn't want to do anything but go to sleep. However, this was her first time here so I gave her the tour. She became excited when she saw the pool for some reason. Afterwards, I made sure the doors were locked and went upstairs to shower. She stepped in with me and both of us stared at one another. We haven't been sexually active in a long time but the chemistry is definitely there.

"Make love to me Alex." Her tongue was in my mouth;

never giving me a chance to respond. I shut the water off, laid her on the bed gently and gave her exactly what she asked for. In return, I received the same.

"Why did you pull out?" I lifted myself up and stared at her.

"I didn't know if you were ready."

"Are you ready?"

"If it's with you, I'll always be ready." We ended up going two more rounds and each time I stayed inside her, letting my sperm find its way to fertilize some more eggs. If she wanted a baby, I'm the only man giving it to her.

****

"You made me breakfast." Gabby had a tray in her hand with a full meal on it.

"Yup because after you eat this food, I'm going to need that mouth somewhere else." I almost choked on the bacon. I moved the tray off my lap.

"Then put your mans favorite meal in his face." She crawled on the bed and stood up. I had my hands on her ass cheeks and went to work pleasing her. She moaned, grabbed my head and shook but the best part of it all is her yelling she still loved me. I know she's said it before but tears fell this time and I knew then, she was the only woman for me.

"I love you so much Alex. I know I pushed you away but you didn't give up on me. Oh my Gawdddddd, I'm cumminggggg." She scratched my back and sucked on my neck.

"I'll always be yours Gabriela Rodriquez." She looked up and smiled when I called her with my last name.

"You want me to have your last name."

"Eventually. You cool with that?"

"I'm not giving this dope dick away for another woman." I stopped in mid stroke to laugh. It made me smile seeing her happy again. I hope the old Gabby I met is resurfacing, because I sure as hell missed her.

We finished pleasing one another, hopped in the shower and headed out to shop. I wanted to show her the mall in San Juan and then have my dad rent a hotel room overlooking the beach. We can't go away too far until all the drama dies down but she'll love it.

"Oh, so this bitch is the reason I haven't been able to see you." I heard and turned around.

"Bitch." Gabby asked and smirked when she turned around to see who it was.

"Baby, I'll let you handle this problem but let her know, your wife is here and she ain't going nowhere." She kissed my lips and walked off. I nodded to one of the security guys to follow her.

"Julia, I told you before we weren't going to be together. Yes, we had fun but I need a woman to settle down with and you're not her."

"After all this time Alex? Why are you treating me like this?" She moved closer and tried to stick her hands down my shorts. I dropped the bags in my hand and tossed her against the wall. I wouldn't put my hands on her because my mom would have a fit.

"Julia you need to listen and listen good. My dick belongs to my future wife. If you ever touch me again, I will cut your fucking hands off."

190

"Alex." She was in shock.

"If you try Gabby in any way, shape or form, I will stab you in the heart and watch you bleed out." She started crying.

"We good baby." Gabby asked and grabbed my hand.

"We good Julia?" She didn't answer.

"I can't hear you. Are we good?"

"Yes Alex." I saw the smirk on my girl's face. I smacked her on the ass and told her to stop being petty. We went into more stores and never ran into Julia again while we were here.

Gabby refused to allow me to buy her anything and kept putting her black card on the counter. A few times, I slipped mine to the cashier when she wasn't paying attention. The good thing about her is, I know she has money but so do I and I enjoy spending it on her.

We were on our way back to my house after spending the night at the hotel, when out of nowhere she bent down and gave me head. I've never had it done by her while I was driving and the thrill of it was even more exciting. I did have to pull over when I was about to cum.

I had her move her seat back and take her pants and panties off. I slid my fingers in and she fucked them as if it were me. I swear the way she moaned out my name and came, I wanted to stop and bend her over the hood of my car.

"You taste good as always." I told her as I sucked my fingers.

"And so do you." I don't know what got into her but she hopped in my lap and rode me while I drove. I don't know how many times I swerved. At least we were by the estate. I parked in the driveway of my house and we both got out.

"Lets go. If you wanted to fuck outside that's all you had to say." I bent her over with her hands on the hood and fucked the shit out of her.

"Yes Alex. Yessssss babyyy." I felt her fluids seeping out and both of our bodies went limp. A nigga was weak. I pulled my pants up and carried her in the house. We left the bags in the car, went inside and fell on the couch. Before I knew it, we were both asleep.

****

"Baby somebody is at your door." Gabby was lying

next to me in just her shirt and bra. I laughed at how she got that way.

"Go take a shower." I smacked her ass and she started whining but got up.

"I want some more of abuela's food. Can you call and tell her we're coming?"

"Anything for you." I watched her walk away and went to my door.

"What the fuck you want?" I asked Joy who stood there with a box in her hand.

"I want to speak to Gabby. Abuela told me she didn't leave."

"For what?"

"It's ok Alex. Let her in."

"I thought you were in the shower."

"I needed a towel and I heard her ask for me." I looked down and she had on a pair of my basketball shorts. Joy stepped in and I closed the door.

"Your ass jiggles in these." I whispered in her ear and squeezed.

"Stop it you pervert."

"I'm the pervert, says the one who gave me some bomb ass head in the car." She covered her mouth laughing.

"I'm not going to stay long. I see you two are making up for lost time." I sucked my teeth.

"I wanted to tell you again, both of you, how sorry I am. It wasn't my intention to do that and I know you both hate me but I brought this for you." She handed Gabby a box.

When she opened it I smiled and my girl started crying. It was a pink bow attached to a headband and a blue boy rattle. There was a nice picture frame and inside was the ultrasound photo of the baby we lost. The last thing she pulled out was a sympathy card.

"How did you get this?" Gabby asked. She was holding the ultrasound photo and wiping her eyes.

"My cousin Ricky is a computer geek and he broke into the files at the doctors office you use and pulled it up. I'm sorry but I didn't know what else to do. When we fought, I wasn't thinking about the baby." I gave her a mean ass look.

"Not like that. What I'm saying is, all I saw was how

you jumped on me. I know you blame me but it's not fair that you're not taking responsibility for hitting me first."

"You pulled a gun on my mother Joy."

"You're right and I shouldn't have but the fact remains that you threw the first punch. I'm not the type of chick who will walk away from it. Again, I am sorry for making you lose the baby. I could've pushed you off or even stopped myself and I didn't."

You're right Joy. I should've never hit you and I didn't see it the way you did. I know you and your mom are a lot tougher than me and mine, but we will always have each others back." Joy nodded her head.

"I know you won't forget but can you forgive me?" Gabby stared at her and then looked at me. I reminded her of what my abuela told her.

"Yes, I forgive you. It may take some time for me to be comfortable around you but I'll get there one day." Joy stood up and gave her a hug.

"I'm sorry Alex. I miss you too."

"I don't miss your ass. Coming over here while I'm

195

trying to make up for lost time. You could've given me a few days to make sure she got pregnant again." Gabby smacked me on the arm.

"What? Shit, as soon as she leave, I'm in it again."

"No. You said we could go get some food."

"Whatever. You done Joy?"

"Alex, stop being mean." Gabby sad but I ignored her.

"I love you Alex and I really am sorry." I gave her a hug.

"If you ever do that shit again, I can promise to disown you, after I fuck you up."

"I won't and stop threatening me. I'm your sister and daddy said.-"

"I know you didn't tell him."

"Yes I did. Alex, you were making me think, you were really going to kill me."

"ALEX!" I shrugged my shoulders and Gabby shook her head laughing.

"Gabby, I hope one day we'll be friends, especially now that I'm expecting with your brother." She had a grin on her face.

"Well you have to get in good with my parents. My mom is going to be happy and she's going to get on your nerves about it. My dad isn't really feeling him right now so I can't tell you what he'd say."

"Its ok. I'm going to get AJ to speak to your dad again. He's taking it real hard not talking to him. He speaks to your mom but your father won't say two words."

"I know. I'm going to have to say something. My dad thinks he chose his friends over us."

"Did he?" Joy asked and stared at Gabby. She had already told me everything that went down at the house the day she lost the baby. From the outside looking in, it did look as if AJ chose us. I know it had to be hard fighting with his pops because they used to be close too.

"He says no but with everything that happened, it seemed that way."

"Well, hopefully he gets up enough nerve to go over there."

"When I go back home, I'm going to set it up. My dad

won't say it, but he misses my brother too."

"Ok Joy, that's enough. I need some alone time with Gabby." I started pushing her out the door.

"Thanks for forgiving me Gabby and I promise to never lie hands on you again. I mean, if I do, I probably won't be alive much longer."

"Long as you know. " I closed the door and went in the living room. Gabby had the ultrasound picture frame in her hand. She handed it to me and asked me to put it on the fireplace along with the rattle and headband. I stood her up and lifted her face.

"You good." I wiped her tears.

"I'm good. Thank you for sticking it out with me."

"Always. You will be my wife one day. Plus, what I look like leaving my baby mama like that?" I carried her upstairs and instead of leaving the house, we ordered food and laid under each other all day and night.

Patience

MJ called and asked me to check on Morgan today because she wouldn't answer his calls or his mom. Of course, I was going to see what was up. She had a breakdown two weeks ago and I could tell MJ was hurting with her. Neither of them told anyone why she was upset but her ass was going to tell me today. My parents had my badass son at the mall with them, so right now is the best time to go.

I didn't bother calling because she's been avoiding everyone. I knocked on her moms' door and waited for an answer. She's being staying here since she gave up her apartment after someone was watching it. Her parents had security over here around the clock. I think that's why my cousin wasn't as worried when it came to her and the baby's safety.

"Hey Patience. She's upstairs." Her mom gave me hug and asked me to get Morgan out the house.

I walked up the steps, opened the door and she was asleep with Le Le next to her. I picked her up and brought her to Morgan's mom and went back upstairs. I opened the curtains, turned the radio on and sat on the bed fiddling with the television remote. She popped up out the bed and looked around, sucking her teeth when she realized it was me.

"Get up. We have a nail and hair appointment in an hour. I also need to stop by the store to pick up something for dinner that you're coming too."

"Not today. I don't feel like leaving the house." She tossed the covers over her head.

"Bitch get your dirty ass up. I don't know what's going on with you but whatever it is, you have to work through it."

"Patience he had a baby on me."

"Say what now?" She sat up in the bed and started explaining everything going on with them. To say I was shocked would be an understatement. MJ, with two baby mamas? Nah, my cousin would never.

"Are you sure?" She wiped the snot coming down her nose with the sleeve of her pajamas and I almost threw up.

"Morgan I'm going to be sick. You know I don't do snot or boogers. Take a shower and we'll talk." I helped her get out the bed and walked her in the bathroom. She turned the water

on and I stepped out to let her handle her business. I changed

the sheets and blankets on her bed, all the while speaking to

MJ and asking what was going on.

"Patience, I swear it's not what it appears to be. I never

cheated on her but it's hard for me to explain how it happened

without feeling like an idiot."

"MJ, whatever went down, you need to tell her. She

loves you and will understand and if she doesn't then maybe

you weren't meant to be together. But you can't allow her to

continue being like this. I had to basically yell at her to leave

the house."

"Oh you got her to leave?"

"Yea. I lied and said we had nail appointments and-"

"Where's the shop?" I told him and he called the place

and they fit us right in.

After we hung up Morgan came out in a towel and I

excused myself while she put clothes on. I wanted to get the

baby ready. Shit, if Morgan was going out, so was she. We can

take turns at the salon watching her. She came downstairs

dressed like her normal self but you could see the bags under her eyes and her skin was pale and saggy like, from not eating. I pray MJ fixed this, because I do not appreciate how my friend is looking.

"Thanks for getting me out sis. It actually feels good." She said as we sat on a bench at a park. After the salon, we shopped for a few and then came out here.

"Morgan, I know you love MJ but you have to get it together. Le Le needs you and this not eating and sleeping all day isn't good for you."

"I know. I just never thought he would have any more kids by someone else. We've gone all these years without each other. Then when we meet up, it's like nothing changed. The love was still there, we had a baby, and BOOM! We get hit with this baby. Never mind he slept with the assistant I warned him about."

"Now you should've smacked his ass for that."

"Nope. I don't do domestic violence. I did tell him I'm going to get his ass back though."

"Shit, you may not do domestic violence but he's a

killer. If you ever decide to sleep with another man, please don't tell me. I need to be as far away from you as possible because he is going to kill you and anyone who knew." We both busted out laughing.

"What are you going to do now?"

"About what?"

"MJ. You know he's not letting you go."

"To be honest, I miss him and I want to go back but he's hiding something. If he can't trust me to understand what it is and that we'll get through it, then I can't be with him. It leaves the door open for him to keep more secrets." I nodded my head and sent a message telling him he had to tell her if he planned on keeping her.

"Well look hussy. What we doing for your birthday?" I knew MJ was planning a surprise party for her. I'm supposed to find us something to do the day of so she wouldn't know he was in town. She was about to speak but I cut her off when this bitch came in my view.

"Get in the car Morgan." I stood up and heard her asking me what was up but my focus was her. I called Alex Jr.

on the phone.

"Get to the park." I didn't have to say which one because it was only one in our area. I hung up, helped her put the baby in the car and walked to where I saw her sitting, pretending shit was good but I had something for that ass. I tapped her on the shoulder. When she saw who I was, a smirk appeared on her face. I couldn't even begin to use my words and started swinging. I grabbed her by the hair and hit her so many times I saw blood leaking. People were yelling and I heard a gun cock on the back of my head.

"Get the fuck off her." I heard his voice and dropped the bitch, but not before kicking her in the face.

"If it isn't the punk motherfucker who thinks he deserves everything and worked for nothing."

"Oh, I'm going to get it and when I do, all of you will be dead and gone."

"You're pathetic. What was my father thinking squirting in your mother?"

"He was thinking how good her pussy was. I mean he did cheat on your mom with her again. Sooooo, I'd have to say he missed her. I spit in his face and I could tell shit was about to go left.

"BITCH!"

"I see no bitches out here, except your mother." I saw Alex Jr. and my cousin Darius standing there with a gun on the back of his head. Instead of CJ dropping his, he turned around and began shooting. I didn't have a weapon on me and had to hit the ground like everyone else and pray I didn't get hit. Somehow, CJ and his mom got away.

"Get home Patience and we'll talk there." Alex Jr. said. Him and Darius had a mean look on their face. I know he's going to rip me a new asshole when I get there. I made my way over to Morgan to make sure she's ok. My phone rang and I hated to answer it.

"ARE YOU FUCKING CRAZY?" MJ yelled in my ear.

"Calm down."

"DONT TELL ME TO CALM DOWN PATIENCE. YOU WERE OUT THERE BEING RECKLESS AS FUCK. MY DAUGHTER WAS IN THE CAR. WHAT WOULD'VE

HAPPENED IF SHE GOT HIT WITH A STRAY?"

"I'm sorry MJ. She started talking shit and-"

"And nothing. That's what's wrong with y'all motherfuckers. You see the person you're mad at and run up on them, not thinking. Shit gets out of hand, like it did, and now look. My daughter and girl could've been hit and you still don't have CJ or his mother. All that shit was for nothing." I didn't say anything and listened to him go in on me.

"Patience how would lil Alex feel if his mom was killed today. Huh?" I just started crying.

"If you ever do some crazy shit like that again around my family; I will fucking kill you. Cousin or not."

"MJ." I heard the two beeping noises and looked at my phone. He hung up on me.

I got to the car and Morgan was in the backseat getting off the ground cradling the baby. Security was helping her out the car. Morgan is far from scary but I saw fear in her face and not for herself but the baby. I was so mad at the bitch; I didn't even think the situation would escalate the way it did. I wanted that woman to die by my hands but today wasn't her day.

"I'll see you later Patience." Morgan got her things out my car.

"Where you going?"

"Home. MJ is having a fit and I just want to get Le Le back to the house."

"I'm sorry Morgan. I didn't know CJ was here and.-"

"I know what's it like to want to kill someone for messing with your family but you have to do it swiftly, without causing a scene. You were messy because your anger overtook your brain and all you saw was red. MJ taught me that, *something can be right in front of us and as bad as we want to touch it, if it's not the right time, you can't. The situation will present itself again and when it does, then you attack.* We all could've been killed Patience." I wiped my eyes because her and MJ were right. I rushed my judgment and the bitch still got away. I hugged her and got in my car. My phone was ringing off the hook from my father. I know someone told him what happened.

CJ

I told Denise, I'd meet her in the park to discuss our plan. She was obsessing over my father who refused to leave CiCi. I told her there wasn't anything she could do to convince him to be with her. Shit, she basically broke in their house; stripped, got her ass beat and he still didn't want her. I'm not sure what my pops had that made women go crazy over him but they were and yet, he still only had eyes for my stepmom. She did leave him over what Denise did but he stalked her until she took him back.

I know people are wondering why I'm coming for my family, when they're the one who took me in. I appreciated how CiCi raised me as her own after finding out she abused my ass for taking a liking to her, but she made me miss out on time with Denise, who is my real mother. I know she was protecting me but when I asked to see her it should've never been a problem.

My mom ended up on drugs real bad and my father didn't try to help or give her money to take care of herself. I

208

think I started hating them more when I turned sixteen and found out they forced Denise to sign over her rights. Again, I'm sure it was for my protection but my dad should've never let it go down. If they had to share custody, then it is what it is.

My brother James Jr. and my cousin Darius now run my fathers empire and it never bothered me because I'm not about the gun life. I wanted it just because I'm the oldest and I would've eventually been ok with it. However, those two didn't want me to have any parts in it. They gave me odd jobs, here and there but I'm not a nickel and dime nigga. Like it or not, Cream is my father and the business always gets handed down to the oldest.

As of lately, Denise told me I should take my spot but I had bigger plans. After MJ knocked me out, all I wanted was revenge. Now his position is where I wanted to be. The empire he had is worth billions and probably trillions, since it's been in their family forever.

Yea, he's my cousin but it don't mean shit. My dad and brothers watched him hit me and did nothing. Motherfuckers praised him like he was a God. I was happy as hell when PJ hooked me up with these Africans who were coming for them. The beef wasn't even with MJ but more so his father and the girls' father, his brother Alex is with.

The plan they had in the works was brilliant and I'm going to be front and center when all these niggas fall and I take the *New Connects* spot on the throne. Yea, I set the shit up the day of his crowning. The owner to the club owed the Africans a favor, which allowed us to get inside.

Unfortunately, he and his family lost their life because of it. Once MJ got to him, they had no chance in the world. Everyone has a price to pay and his family suffered because of it. We did offer protection but no one can really protect you from the Rodriquez family. That's why you had to catch them when they least expect it.

The only one we could get thus far, was my cousin Joy and that's because somehow she left without security. The second time, God was definitely on her side. No one could get to her now because her bodyguards were on point. Alex and MJ were a lot smarter but then again those two don't really need security. They are thorough as hell and the team was too.

"Denise, I told you to pay attention when you were out there." I told her when we got to my house. She has been staying with me ever since. I don't call her mom because of all the time lost. In all honesty, CiCi is my mother.

"Who knew that bitch would be out there?"

"Don't call my sister a bitch." I may not fuck with my family but I loved my siblings more than anything. Just because we're not on the same team doesn't mean anything. My other sister Sienna was my heart too, I guess because she was the youngest.

"How can you defend her after what just happened?"

"What I want to happen doesn't include hurting them. Yea, MJ is our cousin but it's his empire I want." I know I said they would all be dead but my ass ain't killing nobody. Hell, I didn't even like looking at blood.

"Ok but you do know they all have his back and they'll come for you. You need to get Cream on your side. Have him do a sit down with you and MJ; play it cool and then attack." I sat on my couch with my head resting on the back thinking of what Denise said. It could work but then again MJ doesn't care if you're family or not. If you come for him, you can believe he will come for you.

"Pops is not about to help me. He was mad as hell at me for questioning MJ when we were over there."

"Ok and."

"And I had to listen to him go off over it."

"At the end of the day, he is your father. I would hate to think he wouldn't have your back." I picked my phone up and called him just to prove he wasn't with the bullshit. I think it was more or less, of her wanted to hear his voice. I dialed the number and put him on speaker.

"Why the fuck is your disloyal ass calling my phone? Huh? What the fuck are you thinking?" He didn't say hello or how are you.

"Dad, I'm just calling to see if you could get a sit down between him and I to crush this."

"CJ, you are my son and I love you but what you did, put me in a position to choose sides."

"I know you're not about to choose your cousin over your son." My mom yelled in the phone.

"Denise, you are the fucking reason he's in this shit. Had you stayed your stupid ass away, he would've never even thought about coming for MJ."

"Whatever Cream."

"Yea, now its whatever. Denise did you know CJ looked up to MJ and always hung out with him when he was here? Huh? Did you know they spoke on the phone all the time. MJ offered CJ to go over there and he would make sure he had a spot on his team and would want for nothing?" My mom rolled her eyes. I sat there listening to my father break it down on how cool I used to be with MJ. Once she came in my life and started speaking that bullshit, it was as if she were my only family.

"MJ is coming for both of you but I did ask him to make sure your body came to me, so I can give you a proper burial. CJ, I can't believe you let her stupid ass talk you into this shit."

"Dad."

"Goodbye son. I love you." He hung the phone up and I tossed it across the room and watched it crack. My phone rang

213

back but I couldn't see who it was because of what I just did. I answered it anyway.

"Hello." I heard her voice and felt bad instantly.

"CJ, are you ok?" CiCi asked me. I could hear her sniffling.

"I'm good ma." She is the one I called mom. I saw Denise standing there rolling her eyes.

"CJ, I know we've had our issues in the past but you are my son and I care about what happens to you. Why would you go against family honey?" I felt my eyes getting watery and went to my bedroom. I shut the door and fell back on the bed.

"Ma, I don't know. I thought doing this would make her happy."

"Son, she wanted you to do this for her own reasons. We all know she wants your dad and assumed if you were running things, he would be around her. I'm disappointed in you but it doesn't take my love away for you."

"Its too late now ma. I can't do anything about it now."

"I know. I know." I heard her crying and had to move

the phone from my ear. Hearing how upset she was, had me about to cry. When Denise came back in my life, I gave CiCi my ass to kiss. I was disrespectful and ignorant towards her. I made her feel like shit on many occasions in front of people and she still had my back. Now, I'm putting her in a situation to make her bury me.

"Can you come over?" She asked.

"Ma, MJ probably has someone watching and.-"

"He would never come for you in front of your dads house. Sienna wants to see you too." I blew my breath out and told her I would stop by in a few.

I opened my bedroom door and Tara was standing there with a smirk on her face. Yea, she and I have been messing around for a few months. She wanted to get DJ and Zariah real bad for some reason. She never told me why but her brother Armond is coming over to avenge his mom's death as well. She pushed me in the room, slammed the door and stripped out of her clothes.

Tara has some good pussy and she could suck some dick. However, I don't love her and now she's pregnant by me.

215

Yea, I was stupid for running up in her raw and thought it would help me get closer to the crown, by helping them.

It turns out the only one who really had the power to get at MJ and them is the other brother and the chick he's with. PJ is scary as hell and after hearing my cousin Alex knocked him out at the hospital, we all knew he wasn't about that life. How you talk shit to someone and get knocked out?

****

"I'll be back." I told her after getting out the shower. She was lying in the bed watching television.

"Be careful CJ. I don't want anything bad to happen to you." I ignored her and went downstairs to find my mom lying down on the couch.

"Where you going?" She asked as I opened the door.

"Out." I hopped in my car and drove to my parents' house. I saw the two black SUV's rolling behind me and prayed my mom was right about them not attacking at her house. I pulled in the driveway and stayed in my car. I saw my sister Sienna open the door at the same time the SUV's pulled behind my car. She came running to me with tears in her eyes.

"CJ, why would you do that?" She hugged me tight and wouldn't let go.

"I'm sorry Sienna. I was being stupid and.-" I walked in the house and saw my mom sitting on the couch. I could tell she had been crying. I went to hug her and saw MJ standing there with a smirk on his face.

"Ma, you set me up?" She walked over and smacked the shit out of me. I pushed her back and my father had his arms around my neck. I tried to get him to release me but he was too strong. It was a reflex and I didn't mean to touch her.

"James, its ok."

"Nah. Its never ok for him to lay hands on you." MJ said and punched me in the stomach. I heard Sienna screaming.

"James please stop and MJ you too." MJ backed up and my father let go. I hit the floor hard and at the same time gasped for air.

"CiCi, you know I will never allow anyone to put hands on you."

"I know MJ and I love you for protecting me." She kissed his cheek and he gave her space to stand in front of me.

217

My father walked out the room and my sister Sienna followed.

"CJ, like I said on the phone, you are my son and I would never set you up."

"Then why is he here?" I asked still trying to catch my breath.

"When you called and asked your dad to ask MJ for a sit down, he refused so I called him, and luckily, he was in the states already. It took some convincing for MJ to even agree to hear you out but he came on the strength of your father and the friendship y'all used to have. You get here and start making assumptions that are far from the truth and put your hands on me. I may not be your birth mother, but I am your real mother." I put my head down as she went in on me.

"I raised you as my own, without ever raising my hand to you, even after you became disrespectful. I don't want my son to be killed over some power trip he let his birth mother talk him into. I planned on begging MJ not to take you from me. Sienna has been crying her eyes out to your cousin and all you can say, I set you up. Do you hate me that much CJ? Why would you ever think I'd do that to you?"

"I'm sorry ma. Patience and I had it out and.-"

I know and your father, her boyfriend and the rest of us got in her ass over it. CJ, I tried to save you but there's nothing else I can do at this point."

"Ma, you're going to let him kill me." She started crying.

"You did this CJ and I can't keep thinking I did something wrong in raising you."

"MJ, remember what we asked when you're finished." She said and went to walk away. I jumped up and ran after her. MJ stood in front of me. I wasn't going to hit her. I just wanted to hug her one last time.

"I wish the fuck you would touch her." MJ's voice echoed in the house. She walked away shaking her head.

"Get him the fuck out of here." My pops came in yelling after I guess my mom told him what I did. MJ nodded and I was snatched up quick, taken out the house and tossed in the back of the SUV. Two big ass dudes sat on both sides of me. I noticed my father and mom standing at the door with Sienna. I didn't say anything and closed my eyes to mentally prepare myself for what was getting ready to happen. The ride wasn't that long, but long enough. They dragged me out the truck and into some warehouse.

"Well guess who gets to kill the bitch ass son after all?" Patience said when she came out the room. Her boyfriend came out next and then I saw Darius Jr.

I couldn't believe my sister was here to watch me die and possibly be the one to take me out. The door opened and in walked MJ sliding on some black gloves. Someone handed him a small box, which held a small container of liquid. I had no idea what it was and knowing him, it was deadly.

"Don't think I forgot about what your reckless ass did." MJ said to Patience and handed her the bottle.

"I know and I promise to never do it again."

"I'm not worried. You on the other hand should be." She rolled her eyes and her boyfriend shook his head. Next thing I know another door opened and here comes Denise. It looked like someone beat her up again. I stared at Patience and she shrugged her shoulders with a grin on her face.

"CJ, you're going to give this to Denise and afterwards,

we'll deal with you." MJ said standing there.

"Nope. You can do it. I won't be responsible for her death." MJ thought it was the funniest thing ever when I said that.

"Too late cuz. She is the exact reason you are in this situation now. You think she gave a fuck about you." He shook his head no and played a tape recorder.

"CJ is stupid, gullible and will do anything I ask to get in my good graces. Once, I get him on MJ's bad side; he won't have be able to escape his wrath. I want that bitch CiCi gone too, so when Cream mourns, I'll be the one he runs to." I could hear some guy asking her why would she have her own son killed and she told him; I wasn't her son the minute her rights were signed over. I jumped up out the chair and ran over to her, wrapped my hands around her throat and kept choking her.

"You stupid bitch. You made me go against the only real family I had so you could get my father. What the fuck is wrong with you?" I watched her life slipping away and asked Patience for the liquid. I poured it down her throat and almost vomited when I saw what it did to her body.

Her body started shaking and foam began to drip out her mouth. You could see her eyes rolling and all these red marks appeared on her skin. Slowly but surely, her bodily fluids began to leak and it looked like smoke or something came from her pours. Over the next few minutes, I watched her body burn from the inside out and into ashes. I turned around and MJ was staring at his watch.

"Damn, that shit took all of three minutes. Tell dude, I want him to add a little more of the serum to make it go faster." He said to one of his guards.

"Your turn nigga. How you wanna die?" He asked and everyone stared at me. I could beg for my life but my father always told me, not to beg for shit, if I put myself in the situation. I picked the gun up off the table and everyone had a gun on me. MJ crossed his arms in front of him and stood there staring. This nigga ain't scared of shit. I guess he wouldn't be. I'd be dead before I even pointed the gun at him.

"James Jr., tell our parents and Sienna, I'm sorry. I really am and I hope one day y'all forgive me."

"WAIT!" Patience yelled out and ran over crying and

222

hugging me. My brother came over and hugged me too. I was

shocked but at least I know they were with me til the end. I put

the gun back up to my head and pulled the trigger.

"Are you ok?" I asked Morgan when she opened the door. The shit my cousin Patience pulled had me hot and I needed to see for myself that her and my daughter were good. I was on my way here first but CiCi called for CJ, so I made the stop there first, to deal with that shit.

"I'm ok. I was nervous because Arcelia.-" I stopped her from talking by placing a kiss on her lips. Surprisingly she wrapped her arms around my neck and kissed me back. I wasted no time lifting her up and taking her upstairs. This is the first time she allowed me any intimacy since finding out about the other baby and Elaina.

"Who's here?" I removed her shirt.

"Me and the baby." She stepped out her pants and slid on the bed.

"Mmmmm, I missed you so much MJ."

"Damn baby." She was perfectly shaved and some of her nectar seeped out as she laid there waiting for me. My dick tried to fight me to get loose and get inside her.

224

"Let me show you how much." Her hand went in my jeans and set him free. Pre cum was on her fingertips. She put them in her mouth and soon after, I was next.

"Morgan." I moaned out and could care less how much I sounded like a bitch. I've been waiting to be with her and I'm enjoying every moment.

"Do I get to taste you?" She stared up at me with a grin on her face. I nodded and let her take me to a place I haven't been in a long time. I grabbed on to the wall to keep from falling as she sucked, slurped, hummed and did things to my dick that made me fall more in love with her.

"Shit. You're the only woman who makes me feel this good. Damn baby." I helped her off the ground and stuck my tongue in her mouth. Her hands were waking me back up. I pushed her on the bed and was about to dive in but she stopped me.

"MJ, I need to be reconnected to you." I looked at her crazy.

"Do you love me?"

"You know I do Morgan, more than myself."

225

"Then make love to me and make me feel it." I understood what she said but I never felt we were disconnected. Morgan got anything she wanted from me and if this is what she needed, then by all means she's going to get it.

"Relax baby." I told her after I pushed my way in. She was tight as hell from giving birth.

"It hurts."

"You want me to stop?"

"No." It took a few minutes for her to get comfortable. Once she did we were like pornstars again. I had to cover her mouth a few times to keep her from waking my daughter. I needed to make up for lost time and the yelling was not about to stop me. I can't even say how long we were at it but my ass was tired as hell when we finished.

"I love you MJ." My hands were behind my head and she had her chin on my stomach.

"Come home." She smiled.

"You still want me there?"

"You're my wife, well you will be. I want to wake up everyday with you and my daughter."

"Miguel you have another child and.-"

"I didn't cheat on you Morgan. I know it looks that way but I swear it wasn't." I sat up and she was on her knees staring at me.

"Miguel our daughters look to be the same age if I'm going off the photo. How can you have not cheated?" She stood up and put my wife beater on. I grabbed her hand and stood her in front of me.

"Morgan it's hard for me to explain without sounding like a bitch." She lifted my face to make me look at her.

"I would never see you as one no matter what you went through. I've waited years to be with you and as soon as we were living the perfect life, something happened to you that drew us apart. My happiness was snatched from under me and you still won't tell me why. I can't go back with you if.-"

"She put something in my drink and basically had her way with me. I guess she was able to make me cum inside her and it's how the other baby was made." I moved her out the way as she stood there with her mouth hitting the floor. I began putting my clothes on to leave.

"Miguel." She had a sad look on her face.

"I'm over it Morgan." I sat down to put my sneakers on.

"Are you? Because right now you're avoiding me and about to leave. Do you like hurting me?"

"You think I want you hurting Morgan? Huh? The night I choked you, is when I went to tell her to stop calling and texting me. I was on my way out and she passed me a water bottle. I wasn't thinking because the cap was on tight. I finished the water and got dizzy right after. I called Alex to come get me but evidently he didn't get there in time. When he did, she had just gotten off me." She had her hands over her mouth listening to me describe what went down.

"I couldn't even walk out her house Morgan because the shit she put in it, was so powerful, it almost killed me. They said I had foam coming out my mouth and my body was convulsing. Each time you tried to kiss me, all I saw was her. I wanted her dead and at the time, you were her." I could see her crying but I'm not sure why, when it happened to me.

"I'm sorry for everything Morgan but I felt less of a

228

man for getting caught slipping." I walked out the room and into my daughters. I picked her up and she snuggled under my neck like always. I would give my life for her and now if I ever find Carlotta and the baby is mine, I will have two, to do it for.

"Where is she?" I could now see anger in her face.

"Who?"

"The bitch who violated you. I want her NOW!" She shouted waking Arcelia up.

"Morgan."

"Don't Morgan me. Where is your phone? Do you have her number? Is she in Puerto Rico or over here? I'm going to slice her fucking throat." She left the room with my phone and searched all my contacts.

I didn't have any information on her and the numbers she sent the photos from are all pre paids and have been tossed. She was gone in the wind. The sad part is, if the baby is mine, I have no way of finding out. Carlotta knows what she did is wrong and won't ever show her face but I'm missing out at the same time.

I fed, changed, put my daughter back to sleep and went

229

back in the room. I found Morgan sitting on the bed crying. I went over to her and sat down.

"You should have told me Miguel. We missed so much time together over your pride. How could you not tell me?"

"I didn't know how without you thinking it was funny or thinking I wouldn't be able to protect you, if I couldn't protect myself." She sat up and wiped her eyes.

"I would have never thought anything of a sort. You are the man I wanted to marry. The man whose kids I have. The man I grow old with."

"You don't want those things with me anymore. That's why I didn't want to say shit." I stood up.

"Miguel, I want them with you now more than ever because of what you went through. What she did will not break us or keep us apart any longer. I bet she's getting a kick out of knowing we've been separated."

"So what you wanna do?" I asked her.

"I guess take my ass home to my man like he asked." I pulled her close.

"I'm your man again?"

"Not quite. You still slept with that other bitch. I'm gonna need you to come up off her phone number and address too. She'll be getting a visit from me when we touch down."

"Morgan. I haven't messed with her since you left me." She gave me the side eye.

"Ok, I slept with her a few more times but that's it, I swear."

"Good then it won't be a problem when you hear she came up missing." I shook my head laughing. My girl was acting the same way about me, as I do her.

"Is the jet here?"

"Yea."

"That's even better. The faster I fuck her up, the better. The bitch knew she wanted you and.-" she stopped pacing and looked at me.

"I should fuck you up for letting her have my dick. Lucky for you, I'm in a good mood."

"This is a good mood. I hate to see you in a bad one."

"Don't play with me MJ."

"Oh now I'm MJ."

"You'll be whatever I want, but you'll be mine so it doesn't matter."

"Always Mrs. Rodriquez. Always." We engaged in a passionate kiss, then I helped her finish packing; not that she needed anything. I was happy as hell to bring my woman and daughter home. She could've left in the t-shirt she had on and I'd be fine.

Morgan

I've been back in Puerto Rico for a week and Miguel hasn't left my side. Besides taking care of Arcelia and sexing each other down, neither of us went anywhere. I stared down at him as he slept with my daughter on his chest. I snapped a photo, put it as my screensaver and began putting my clothes on.

Joy and Ricky would be here in ten minutes and told me I better be ready. Yes, the three of us had become tight since I've been with Miguel.

"Call me when you're through so I can send someone over there to clean the mess you fools make." He said. I thought his ass was asleep but I guess not. He placed Le Le on the bed and rolled over making sure he didn't wake her. I walked over to him and kissed his neck.

"How do you know what I'm about to do?" He turned to look at me.

"I'm going to tell you what my father told my mom anytime she tried to be sneaky."

"And what's that?" I folded my arms.

"Nothing gets passed me baby. Everything you do or wanna do, I know about it or will. Now, like I said, "Call me when you're done."

"I know, I know. You'll send someone to clean up." He hopped out the bed and ran over to me as I headed out the door.

"Morgan don't get fucked up."

"You can't beat me."

"Oh I can't." He lifted me on his shoulders and ran down the steps with me yelling. He threw me on the couch and plopped on top of me. He had my hands above my head and slid my leggings down along with my panties.

"Who can't beat who?"

"Ahhh fuck Miguel. You know I have to be ready in a few minutes. Shit baby." I lifted my legs and let him continue taking care of my body. We heard banging at the door and Ricky outside talking shit.

"Let them wait. Ride me baby."

"Miguel." He sat up and tossed me on his lap." We

234

stared in each other's eyes as I mounted myself on top. He put the throw blanket around my waist and grabbed a hold of my hips.

"Give me my son Morgan." I shook my head yes and kissed him aggressively. That's all I could do as the orgasm had me shaking like a leaf.

"I can't stand y'all. Joy, they in here fucking." I heard Ricky say. We were so into it; neither of us paid attention to the alarm when it announced who came in.

"Don't stop Morgan until I put my son in you." Ricky slammed the door when he walked out and Miguel and I continued as if they weren't waiting.

"I love the fuck out of you Morgan. Shit, this pussy good."

"I love you too baby. I'm about to cum. Yes baby, yes." I shouted and he came right behind me. We sat there staring at one another.

"You're going to be my wife soon." He pushed my hair back.

"I'm not in a rush baby. Whenever you're ready, I'll be

right here. Come take a quick shower with me." I lifted myself off him and felt both of our juices sliding down my leg. He stood up and carried me upstairs. I threw something on and ran out the house before I got caught up with him again.

"It's about time. Damn." Ricky said when I got in the car. Joy backed out snickering.

"Both of y'all know, when my man wants it, he gets it." I rolled my eyes.

"Ok, but you live there. He could've waited until you got home." Ricky said snapping. I paid his ass no mind because he was always extra. I know he wouldn't dare talk this shit in front of Miguel.

"Whatever." Joy drove and twenty minutes later, parked at what I'm assuming is a warehouse but it was huge. I wasted no time going in to get this bitch.

"Please don't kill me. I'll do whatever." Elaina yelled out when she saw me.

"I hate when a bitch begs for her life." I walked over and punched her so hard in the face, her nose cracked instantly.

"I told you to stay away from my man."

"I did. He wanted me." She cried as her nose leaked.

"So him being drunk and asleep in his office, was him wanting you. Or was that his way of telling you to suck his dick to wake him up. I mean, most people that are drunk and asleep, don't even know what's going on until its too late."

"Oh shit bitch. Only his woman supposed to get him up like that. Fuck that bitch up Morgan." Ricky said.

"I'm sorry."

"People are always sorry when they get caught but let me ask you this." I put my face in front of hers so that we were eye to eye.

"Was it worth your life?" She didn't say anything.

I told Ricky to hand me the bucket of acid I asked him for when we first got here. Joy handed me a pair of gloves to wear so it wouldn't spill on me by accident. I took a mixing cup and scooped out a little and let it fall on her feet. The smoke or whatever that is when it hits the skin, started coming out. She started screaming.

"Not only did you do that but you continued sleeping with him. Then you told everyone he was your man." I let acid fall down her kneecaps and watched them detach from her body. The shit was pretty gross to be honest.

"Please stop. I'm pregnant." All of us stared at her.

"By who? I know my man isn't that stupid to run up in you raw." She shook her head no and passed out. I guess the melting of her skin did something to her. As long as it wasn't Miguel's baby, I could care less. But then again she wouldn't have it anyway. I grabbed the knife out of Ricky's hand and slit her throat from ear to ear. I was making sure this bitch never woke up.

"You should've made her suffer a little more." Joy said tapping away on her phone.

"She passed out. I doubt if she was going to wake up from it. Don't worry because when I find Carlotta, that bitch will definitely wish she was never born." They both looked at me.

"Yes, he finally told me." I said.

"Its about damn time. He was walking around with a chip on his shoulder." Ricky said and sucked his teeth.

"I know. He was worried I wouldn't think he could protect me, if she got him."

"Damn, my cousin is really in love. You must have some fire ass pussy."

"That's something you or no other man will ever know about her." Miguel said stepping in and mushed the shit out of Ricky, who started swinging his arms like a windmill with his dramatic ass.

"MJ, you can beat all those other motherfuckers but you got no win here. Put your hands on me again." Ricky was pressing his luck. Miguel removed his phone and the necklace he had on and handed it to me.

"Nigga, I was just playing." Ricky said when he noticed my man was serious.

"That's what the fuck I thought." I handed him his stuff.

"Punk ass." Ricky shouted and ran to the other side of the warehouse.

"I'm going to make sure Ryan beats your ass later." Ricky gave him the finger. He walked up behind me and looked on the ground.

"Damn baby. You did some damage." He had his face frowned up at the remains of her body.

"That's right. She should have listened when I gave her a warning. Your ass is next."

"You can try but then this dick won't be around."

"Yes it will."

"How you figure?" He placed kisses on my neck.

"I'll cut it off when you're asleep, have it stuffed and put on my night stand. He lifted his head and stared at me.

"Yea, they're rubbing off on you. Stay away from my wife you two."

"Don't put me in it." Joy said putting her hands up.

"MJ, you know I'm using a blow torch to Ryan's manhood if he ever cheats again. Fuck you think this is? I told her, your ass needed to suffer too." Ricky said making us all laugh.

"I need to suffer Morgan?"

"I think you already have when I left you."

"You damn right I did and don't do that shit again."

"Don't give me a reason to."

"I won't." He took my hand in his and we all headed towards the door. The Pablo guy came in to clean up the mess I made.

"You riding home with your man." Joy asked.

"I guess. Who has Le Le?" I looked at Miguel who was telling the guy to make sure its cleaned up well.

"I had Mariana come over. You know she thinks Arcelia is her baby anyway." I laughed because his sister was always over now or she would take her as soon as we walked in his parents' house.

"Did you drive?" He took my hand in his.

"Yea why?"

"Because I love riding you as you're driving." He stopped for a second and turned around to see where everyone else was.

"Then what you waiting for? My man is always ready for you." He opened the door, sat down, undid his jeans and had me climb on top.

"Can't y'all wait to you get home?" Ricky said riding by sticking up his middle finger. Luckily, the door was closed or he would've damn sure got a peek of my goodies. I guided myself down and began sucking on his neck. He was not small and I always had to get used to it first.

"You ready ma?" He started the car.

"Yes. Are you?"

"Yup. I'm going to make sure my son is in you every chance I get." He pulled off and I gave him exactly what he wanted. We almost crashed twice but it was well worth it. The way we had each other moaning, I don't ever want to think of another man. MJ is the only man I ever want touching my body and as long as his cheating ways are over, he will be.

Aiden (AJ)

When Joy announced to her pops she was pregnant and the baby was mine, I damn near jumped out my seat. Not only is she his favorite but he knows I touched her. I wanted to stay to make sure she was good, however, my sister was too upset.

Gabby has gone through a lot and being in P.R. with the exact people who caused her to miscarry is a bit much. I give it to Alex though, that nigga really loved my sister. He came to the airport to get her and said he wasn't leaving without her. I thought she wouldn't go but I saw the love in her eyes too.

I hopped on the plane and thought about how over the last year all of our lives have been turned upside down, due to beef with our fathers and my stupid ass cousin, getting Tara pregnant. Why he slept with her period is beyond me, when she's younger than him. Age shouldn't matter but Tara was one of those young, dumb, immature, ghetto bitches you try and stay away from.

244

The day we found out, is the day my pops disowned me.

The shit has been bothering me for weeks now, yet, I couldn't

make my way over to apologize. I knew I was wrong but my

dad ain't nothing to fuck with. If Gabby said he's still pissed,

it's best I stay away.

My mom reached out to me and we speak just about

everyday but my father had no words for me. However, my

mom was coming over to make me dinner because she misses

all of us being together. I started straightening up when I heard

the doorbell.

"Mmmmmm. Damn, I see you missed me." I said to

Joy after we separated from our kiss. I locked the door and she

followed me in the living room.

"I did baby and I'm sorry for ambushing you like that

over my parents house. Let me make it up to you." She didn't

give me a chance to do anything and pulled my jeans and

boxers down.

"Fuck Joy. Damnnnnnnn." Are the only words I could say. She deep throated me so good, my ass was moaning.

"As bad as I want to taste you, I've been needing to feel you." After she got comfortable and slid all the way down, we went at it in the living room. I took her to the bedroom and we finished in the shower.

"You good." I asked putting on some clothes. I looked over at her and she was lying there dosing off.

"I love you Joy and I'm happy you're having my baby."

"I love you too AJ. I'm scared and excited."

"Don't be. I know you and my baby won't want for shit but just know, I got you for whatever." She sat up and we kissed again.

"My mom is coming to make me dinner."

"Ok. I'll be up here until she leaves."

"Joy don't do that."

"AJ, after what happened, she may not want to be around me. I'm ok though. Just make me a plate."

"Nah. You're not eating unless you come get it." She poked her lips out and I stepped out the room. I went to finish straightening up before my mom saw the mess we made. Joy's clothes were on the floor and so were mine. I felt her hands behind my waist and her head on my back. I turned around and smiled.

"You can't come down here like that and expect me to be ok." Joy was ass naked standing in front of me. My dick sprang to life. She jumped in my arms and just as I laid her down the doorbell rang. She took off upstairs with me laughing. That's what her nasty ass gets.

"Mommy said help her get the bags out the car." Gabby said coming in with Alex strolling behind her with a few bags.

"Ma, why you buy all this food?" She had a trunk full of groceries.

"Because everyone is coming over and I need to feed them all." She walked away and left me standing there with my mouth opened. Alex came back out shaking his head laughing.

"What?"

"Nothing man. Tell my sister she can come out of hiding."

"How you know she here?"

"You know better than that but if you're going to have her here, at least let her clothes and shit be out of the area we're all going to be in." He started grinning. I walked in and sure enough her things were still on the floor. I was in the process of picking all her stuff up at the time but she distracted me.

"GET DOWN HERE JOY!" I heard my mom yell. I stared at Gabby and she shrugged her shoulders. Joy came down in some leggings and a long shirt.

"Please don't leave anymore hickeys on her neck like that. I know she's having your baby but she's still my baby." I turned around and her father was standing there.

"DADDY!" She shouted and ran to him. What the hell is going on? He started speaking in Spanish to her and pointing at her neck.

"AJ." Mrs. Rodriquez said and stepped in with MJ, Morgan, their daughter and before I could shut the door, DJ, his girl and family came in. I don't know what my mom did, but what the hell?

"AJ, it's time." My mom said and walked me outside. My dad was leaning against a car smoking with my uncle. They both stared at me and my mom squeezed my hand.

"You gonna stand there looking stupid or hit this?" My dad said and passed me the blunt.

"Aiden, I swear if you blow that in my face, you won't get none for a month." He started coughing and grabbed my mom from behind.

"You good nephew?" My uncle asked as I watched my parents gush over one another.

"Yea. I'm sorry unc. I never chose.-" He put his hand up.

"You don't have to convince me. I know everyone's emotions were high but you were wrong for leaving. Your mom was hurt and my brother has been fucked up over hitting her. You may think it's his fault but you getting in your moms face the way you did, made him react that way. He's your father AJ and despite what you think, he'll never allow anyone to fuck with his family or you; regardless of what happened."

"Huh?" Now I was confused.

"When you went to P.R. He knew and made sure to have someone watching you. He was still mad but it will never make him stop protecting you."

"I didn't know."

"Listen. Your father is very hotheaded and he doesn't care about power or who has what. If you fuck with his family, he's going to come for you."

"Daddy, I thought you were going to be with me all day." Gabby said coming out the door like she had an attitude. My father spoiled the fuck out of her. Here she had Alex and still wanted my dads attention.

"I'm coming Gabby. I had to say a few things to your mom." He placed a kiss on my moms' lips and she went in the house, taking my sister with her.

"I'm sorry pops. I know it looks different but I never chose anyone over my family. I'm sorry for standing in front of mom and making you think otherwise. I know it's my fault you hit her too because had we not been arguing, it would've never happened. I miss you pops." He hugged me and told me I better not ever let shit go down like that again.

"Did you make up with your dad?" Joy asked when we walked in.

"Yea."

"Good because you missed him. Your mom threatened me though." She shrugged her shoulders.

"What you mean?"

"She said I better not hurt you and that she expects to see her grandbaby at least every other weekend." We both busted out laughing and joined everyone in the living room. So far everything seemed to be back to normal, but I'm sure something else will kick off soon.

Gabby

It was nice to have everyone sitting around enjoying themselves, without arguing and guns being drawn. I'm really happy my dad and AJ are speaking and so is my mom. I overheard her tell my dad, she has a surprise for him at home. He was happy and told her they could leave now. I loved the way they loved on each other and hoped to have that when I get older.

I noticed Alex's mom staring at me and began to feel uncomfortable. It wasn't that I was scared but she has a way of intimidating the hell out of you with her eyes. She stood up and asked me to meet her outside. I noticed my mom got up and so did everyone else.

His mom told them to relax and my mom told her she was still coming. Alex wasn't sitting down either and followed. We only went in the den and big Miguel told his mom, she better leave the door opened. After she sucked her teeth, Alex asked her what did she want.

"First off, I want to apologize to you and your mom for what went down a while ago. Tempers flared, we laid hands on each other and a child was lost in the process." I put my head down.

"Ma, I'm going to ask you to stop bringing it up."

"I had to apologize son. Anyway Gabby, I don't appreciate the way you spoke to me but I respect it." Alex had a smirk on his face.

"No one has ever been bold enough to come at me or even swing." She looked at my mom.

"However, you and my son are together and from the glow around you, it's safe to assume you'll be expecting again." Alex snapped his head.

"Baby, I literally just found out." I took him in the bathroom and pulled the test from under the sink. I had it wrapped up in tissue and planned on bringing him in to see it later. He lifted my chin and kissed me. It was intense and erotic, just the way I like it. I didn't care who was in the other room. I wanted him right now. I began to unbuckle his jeans but he stopped me.

"I got you later baby." He said when I almost got them down. He opened the door and held my hand on the way out.

"I thought you knew Alex. I'm sorry." His mom said.

"It's alright ma. Are you finished?"

"No. I wanted you to have this Gabby." She handed her a gift bag. Inside of it was a baby book to keep record of our baby's life. I guess she knew I'd be getting her pregnant again. A pink and blue blanket knitted together and an envelope. She opened it and there was a four-digit number on it.

"I don't know what this number means."

"It means you are welcomed on the estate anytime you want. That's the code to the front gate."

"Really!"

"Alex said he's going to marry you, so I may as well give it to you."

"Thank you Mrs. Rodriquez and I'm glad we can move past what happened. I really love Alex and I didn't want him to always have to see me here." I gave her a hug and we heard someone clapping. Big Miguel walked in smiling.

"Look at my wife apologizing on her own. I'm proud of you baby." He stood behind her and whispered something in her ear.

"Ok now that this is over, can I get my moment?" MJ asked and we all followed him in the dining room.

"Morgan." He called out and asked her to stand up.

"Oh my God. Is he about to.-"

"Be quiet Gabby." I covered my mouth and watched her go to him. He took her hand in his and got down on one knee. Instantly, everyone began taking their phone out to record, including me.

"Morgan, we have known each other for quite some time now. We lost touch for a few years but the moment we reconnected, it was as if the love grew stronger. When you said you we're going to ride with me, I didn't know you really meant it. The love I have for you is so strong; you'll never have to worry about anyone taking me from you. I don't see anyone but you and I put that on my life." Morgan had to wipe her eyes over and over from the massive amount of tears falling. Shit, she had all the women shedding some.

"You are the true definition of a rider, and stuck by me through some rough times and I love you even more for it. I promise not to ever cheat or make you question your place in my life. You have my daughter and hopefully my son is in there. There's no other chick out here who can handle me or my lifestyle; except you. You don't let me treat you like shit and you hold down the home front. I love the hell out of you. Will you marry me?" She nodded her head. He slid the ring on her finger and I'll be damned if the rock wasn't huge. I thought about the song upgrade you when Jay Z said, the ring so big it won't fit in her new purse. The shit was so big; I didn't even have to get near to see it.

"Close your mouth Gabby. I'll make sure you have a big one too." He pushed my chin closed.

"No thank you. That's too big."

"Fine. I'll get you one out the Cracker Jack box." I punched him in the arm. MJ and Morgan were still kissing so everyone left them standing there. We all went in the living room and the guys went outside to talk or smoke.

Morgan finally came in after a while. If you ask me, I think they had sex in one of the rooms. We left them in the dining room but they came from upstairs. AJ had a set of stairs in the kitchen that led to the second floor. He said when he's hungry; he should have steps that led straight to the kitchen. *Lazy ass*!

We congratulated both of them but he left out in a hurry. Joy asked what was wrong but she said, it's something he had to take care of ASAP. I wanted to know but decided against asking her. A few minutes later Alex came in and told me he had to go back to P.R. with MJ. What the hell was going on?

****

I didn't speak to Alex for the next two days and a bitch was stressing. His phone went to voicemail each time and when I asked AJ to ask Joy if he was ok, he told me, he's fine. They're handling family business. I was worried but not too bad because their security is out the ass.

"What up Gabby?" Tara asked coming towards me with a big belly. I had stopped by the seven eleven to grab a Slurpee and baby magazines.

"You're pregnant again?" I asked. I didn't mean to sound judgmental but my cousin Jacob is barely one.

"Yup and it's by CJ's before you ask." She rubbed her belly as if it were cute.

"Does he know?"

"Yes he does. I thought you were expecting." I gave her a funny look because who would tell her? Then again CJ is Alex's cousin.

"Unfortunately, I lost it."

"I'm sorry Gabby. I didn't know." She seemed genuinely concerned but I couldn't say if she were.

"Thank you." I put my things on the counter.

"Why did you sleep with my cousin? You knew he was with Zariah?" She had a sneaky grin on her face.

"Everything happens for a reason."

"Excuse me. Tara, don't tell me you did it on purpose. I mean what would be the reason?"

"Fuck Zariah. She thinks she's better than me but guess what, she's not. I got something from him first to make her hurt, the way me and my brothers hurt. It may not be the same but its close enough." She dropped the items in her hand and stormed out.

The cashier looked at me and I shrugged my shoulders. What could Zariah possibly have done spiteful enough to make Tara jump on my cousin? Yes, I say Tara initiated it because Akeem isn't like that. Shit, Zariah had to come on to him, in order for him to even attempt to go out with her.

I got in my car and felt as if someone was watching me. I made sure all my doors were locked and glanced around the parking lot.

Knock! Knock! I heard on the side of my window and looked up into the eyes of PJ. He was standing there looking good as hell. I rolled my window down and asked him what he wanted. But before he could answer a black SUV pulled into the parking lot and almost ran him over. Some big guy jumped out and came over in our direction. PJ asked if I knew him and I told him no.

"Go home Gabby."

"Huh? Who are you?"

"Yea, who the fuck are you?" PJ said and a few of his boys came from out of nowhere. This trip to the store was about to turn into a nightmare.

"Don't question him Gabriela, just go." I heard on the speakerphone.

"Alex!"

"Who else would it be? Never mind that, go home. I'll call you in a few."

"No. I was talking to PJ. I haven't spoken to you in days and you expect me to.-"

"Take me off speaker phone and hand it to her."

"Alex, how dare.-" Again he cut me off.

"Gabriela, if you're going to be my woman you need to listen to what the fuck I say. If I'm telling you to leave its for a good damn reason. Now pull the fuck off."

"Who are you talking to?"

"I'm talking to you." I took the phone away from my ear because I couldn't believe he was this angry, when he's the one who hasn't contacted me.

"Look, I know you're not used to hearing me speak this way to you but you're in the middle of some bullshit right now. And you let him know I'm not in town."

"What are you talking about?"

"Gabby, never discuss my absence in front of a nigga who one...still wants you and two... is there for a reason. Do you honestly think he just popped up? Huh? I bet he's smiling in your face right now." I looked up and he was outside my car with his arms folded and smirking.

"Exactly! Now go home and I'll call you shortly." He hung up and I started my car.

"Oh, so I can't tell you what to do but he can. He's no better than me Gabby and when he breaks your heart too, if he already hasn't, I'll still be here. Keep thinking that nigga faithful. " PJ said and the dude told him to keep it moving. I don't know what happened after that because I pulled off. I couldn't help but think of what my ex said. Is Alex trying to run my life? Will he hurt me? Shit, is he cheating? I had so many thoughts going on in my head; I didn't realize someone ran a red light until it was too late.

Zariah

"I'm here cuz, give me a second." I told Alex and walked up to the nurses' station. Alex called me up and told me something happened to Gabby. I shot up out of bed and woke Akeem up. I had him call his aunt, who is her mom and let them know she was hurt. No one knew what happened and right now, Akeem and I are the only ones here.

"Excuse me. My cousin was brought in and.-" The nurse put her finger up to tell me one minute. I sat there listening to her discuss something about another patient, which as an upcoming doctor, she shouldn't be doing.

"What she say?" Alex asked in the phone.

"Nothing because she won't get off the phone."

"MJ, I need you to handle something." I heard him say and he hung up. Not even a minute later the nurse looked at the phone and kept pressing the receiver as if something was wrong with the phone. She hung it up and had the nerve to say she'll be right back. I snatched her by her arm and pushed her against the desk.

"First of all, you had no business discussing a patient in front of me. You violated all types of confidential and privacy laws doing it." I could see the nervousness in her eyes. People got fired all the time for what she did.

"Second, I asked if my cousin were here and I expect for you to look." She ran around the desk and asked for her name. I gave it to her and she pressed the button for the back door to open.

"My aunt and uncle will be here in a few minutes, they are her parents. If they tell me you gave them a hard time, I promise to come back and finish what I started." I mushed her upside the head and shoulder checked her on the way to the back. Motherfuckers working these nurses' stations need to be trained better. My phone rang and it was Alex.

"I'm walking in now."

"Alex, there's doctors in the room with her. Hold on." We stood outside and waited for them to come out. Her parents came running over and so did AJ, Joy and DJ.

"What happened? Are they saying anything?" Her mom asked.

"No we just got here too."

"Fuck this." Her dad said and walked in the room. You could see one of the doctors speaking with him and a few minutes later he came out.

"Is she ok?" Her mom tried to look in the room but they had the curtain blocking.

"She was in a car accident. She hit her head and he said it looks as if her arm is broke. They are checking on the baby and are going to send her down for a CAT scan too."

"Is she awake?" AJ asked.

"No." Her dad was pacing back and forth.

"FUCKKKKKK!" He father yelled out and punched a hole in the wall.

"Is that her father?" I heard Alex ask.

"Yes."

"This ain't no fucking accident."

"Aiden, don't say that." Arizona was crying and everyone else stared at Aiden.

"Ari, I may be out of the game but this is not an accident. Someone did this to her and I'm going to find out who it is." He stormed off and Arizona asked the guys to follow him. I don't think I've ever seen him that upset.

"MJ and I are on the way. Tell her mom not to worry. When he steps out the hospital, someone will be watching to make sure he's good. Zariah please don't leave her."

"I won't. Just get here. You know she's going to want you,"

"I know and thank you for going."

"We family Alex and you know we're all we got. Love you and be careful getting here." We hung up and I sat down next to Arizona and Joy who looked nervous about being around her. I guess after making Gabby lose the baby she was still uncomfortable.

"Why is all this happening to her?" I don't know but we're going to find out.

We sat there for hours waiting for them to let us see her. She was still asleep because they gave her some medicine to sedate her until they finished all the tests. Alex walked in the hospital with MJ and he looked like he was in rare form.

I could tell by his demeanor that he was about to lose it when he saw her. Gabby had a soft cast on her arm, a bandage on her head because she had to get a few stitches for the gash and her face had bruising on it.

"God, please don't take her baby again. Zariah, she won't be able to take it, if it happens again."

"Did something happen to my baby?" Alex said and her mom stood up and hugged him.

"We don't know yet. They let us see her for a few minutes but no one has said much about the baby."

"Fuck this." Alex, walked over to the doctor who was sitting at the desk, yoked him up, made him go in the room and give a full run down of what happened to Gabby.

"How is my baby?" The doctor was scared as hell.

"The baby or should I say babies are fine."

"Say what?" All of us had our mouths on the floor.

"We did an ultrasound before she went for the CAT scan and there were two heartbeats. I apologize for not mentioning it but some guy named MJ called threatening to blow the hospital up if I told anyone. I figured once he got here, we'd tell him." We all started laughing as MJ shrugged his shoulders.

"He told me on the phone. I wanted to see your face when he told you."

"If her mom wasn't here, I'd cuss you out."

"Go ahead Alex. Shit, I've been sitting here worried and he knew." Alex went in on MJ in Spanish and all we did was laugh. The good thing about it, is he didn't get mad and apologized to Alex.

"Where is she?" We turned around and PJ walked in with his dirty ass sister and their mom. I know this bitch ain't pregnant again. I looked at Akeem and he swore it wasn't his this time.

"Zariah, we are at the hospital and hopefully you're pregnant. Remember, you're going to be a doctor." Akeem whispered in my ear as he held me by the waist. Alex made this cynical laugh as he walked up on PJ.

"Why you here my nigga? Did you have something to do with this?"

"Says the motherfucker who let her come out at night by herself. How you questioning me and your punk ass was in another country doing shit with your ex." All of us stood there quiet.

"Yea, you thought no one knew what you did." PJ had a smirk on his face.

"You were with Julia, Alex." We all turned around and Gabby was awake on a stretcher.

"It wasn't like that."

"You left me alone to be with her."

"Gabby, let me explain."

"No. There's no reason you can give me on why you were with her. I know it's not your fault what happened to me, but maybe if you were here, I wouldn't have been out the house. Or maybe I wouldn't have to listen to my ex tell me in so many words you weren't faithful. I guess he was right when he said, I don't know what you're doing over there."

"Yea nigga, explain how you were at your ex's house in the middle of the night." All hell broke loose after that. Alex was beating the shit out of him and MJ dared anyone to contact the cops or even break it up. Tara and her mom were screaming like maniacs and once my parents walked in, it was as if they seen a ghost. MJ pulled Alex off and PJ's ass appeared to be dead.

"What the fuck are you doing here?" My mom asked Tara's.

"Well, well, well. If it isn't the stuck up, Heaven Martin."

"Hold up. How do you know my mother?" I stepped in front of her, blocking my mom.

"Oh we go way back, don't we?"

"Ma, what is she talking about?"

"Another time Zariah. How is Gabby?"

"Get these motherfuckers out of here." Alex barked and their security dudes began escorting them out. One dragged PJ by his feet because he was knocked out.

"She's fine as far as her accident but mentally, I don't know. But dad how do you two know them?"

"What did your mother say Zariah?" I put my head down and walked away. I hated secrets and they knew it, yet, neither of them decided to tell me shit.

"You good baby?" Akeem had my hand in his and sat by me outside on the bench.

"I don't know. We are getting hit from so many directions and then, I find out my parents somehow know who PJ's family is."

"Zariah, whatever it is, will come out. Let's go home so I can release some of your stress." He carried me to the car and once we got home, he definitely released any stress and anger I had. Damn, I loved this man.

****

"I'm going to pick Jacob up." I told Akeem on the way out.

He was supposed to get him but he hated going over there. The one time he did break down and go, Tara tried to fuck him. Yes, pregnant and all. By the time I got over there to put my foot off in her ass, she was pulling off. I sent her a threatening text message and I bet her ass won't pull that shit

273

again. I could've called but I wanted to make sure she at least read it. You know when you're arguing, people tend to over talk or hang up on you.

I parked in front of her house and sure enough it was a few niggas outside. The cute one I met when I first came here, stared at me with lust in his eyes. I swear if I weren't with Akeem, I'd definitely give his ass a run for his money. He licked his lips and instead of turning my head, I gave him a wink. I stared him up and down and took my ass inside before I got in trouble.

"Tara, this bitch here." Soon as I heard her mom say that, I yoked her up.

"You don't know me well enough to call me out my name. I haven't done anything to you or your daughter, yet, but you keep talking, I'll give you her beat down."

"Whatever, you just worry about making sure you take good care of your cousin tonight." I let her go.

"What the fuck are you talking about? Jacob is my boyfriends son." She started laughing hysterically.

"I guess your parents didn't tell you."

"Zariah." I heard my moms voice outside. I went to the door and saw both of my parents.

"Ma, what are you doing here?" My dad got out the truck with her.

"We came to your house and Akeem mentioned you were coming here."

"Too late Heaven. I already told her Jacob is her cousin." The blood drained from my moms face and that shit made me nervous.

"Ma, what is she talking about?"

"Zariah, get Jacob and lets go. We'll talk at the house."

"Nah, I think you should tell her now." PJ said.

"OH MY GOD!" My mom covered her mouth and backed up. My dad looked at PJ and shook his head. They didn't get a good look at him in the hospital because his face was busted up. But how did they know him to begin with?

"That's right Heaven. He looks just like his father."

"Ma, what the hell is going on?"

"Day, take me home please." My mom turned to get in the car.

"No. I want to know how you know each other."

"PJ's father is your mom's ex."

"Ok so what." I said still confused listening to Tara's mom speak.

"Your parents killed my pops. His name was Polo and guess what? Your father and my father were first cousins, so it looks like we're related. Meet Polo Jr. bitch." Tara said with a smirk on her face.

"Ma, not the Polo who beat you so bad, he almost killed you." I didn't mean to tell her business but it slipped out.

"Don't speak ill of the dead Zariah. We all know it wasn't true." My mom walked up on their mom.

"Candy, you watched him beat on me at the engagement party you showed up to. You remember the one where he was announcing to everyone how he was giving me his last name and not you."

"Whatever."

"Yea, its whatever now, but you thought it was funny how he almost killed me in front of all those people. If it hadn't been for my husband, I'd be dead." Candy threw her head back laughing.

"Oh yea, the cousin who was sleeping with his girl. Only ho's do that. I mean what woman sleeps with her own man's cousin and has a baby by him. Did you expect him not to want to kill you? Oh and lets not forget how your perfect husband cheated on you with Asia over and over, and you killed her." My mom had tears in her eyes. I think that struck a nerve with because my mom was so in love with my dad and to this day, I had no idea he cheated on her.

"I can see you're upset because Zariah is hearing all the bad shit you've done. The anger you're showing right now, only proves that you know, you weren't shit. And to think, regardless of how bad Polo beat on you, you were still the only woman who had his heart." My mom stood there crying and my dad was pissed. He yoked Candy up and his boys came around my dad.

I tried to speak but no words would leave my mouth. How am I going to deal with knowing my fiancé's son is really my cousin, how the hell did I not know? Why didn't my

277

parents tell me? I went to step off the porch and everything

went black.

MJ

"Is everything in place?" I asked Alex who had just come back from the states. He was in hot water with Gabby over the bullshit PJ said. Yes, he was over here with Julia but like my brother said, it had nothing to with him sleeping with her.

We found out she had been in contact with some people and was trying to have Gabby killed. She was obsessed with my brother and refused to allow him to be happy. Unfortunately for her, she forgot who we were. The same person she asked to commit the murder, is the same guy who worked for us.

See everyone assumed we had lieutenants and didn't know who was on our team. That's never the case. Anyone hired to join anything with the name Rodriquez on it, had to be checked out thoroughly. I'm talking about parents, grandparents, ancestors, friends, foes and anyone else affiliated with them.

A few times we went to the their houses if they had dogs to see how certain individuals handled them. Are they friendly with their pets or abusive? Shit, like that can tell a lot about a person. It may sound crazy but the way people take care of animals can show how they are in situations too.

"Yea. You ready." I stood up and grabbed my things to leave.

"What you going to do now that you found out it's true? You think Morgan will be ok?" I ran my hand over my head.

"I don't know but one thing I know for sure, is her ass ain't leaving me." He nodded his head and sat back staring out the window. I removed my phone out my pocket and looked at the text.

Wife: *I can't wait to see you. I miss you.* Morgan was still in the states visiting her family, who was ecstatic when they found out I proposed.

Me: *I miss you too.* I opened up the next message and was blown away. Morgan had on a one-piece lingerie set with some fuck me heels on. Her leg was on a chair and her fingers were in her pussy. I got a video right after and there was no way in hell, I could open it with my brother sitting next to me.

Me: *Bring that ass home TONIGHT!* I put the phone in my pocket when the truck came to a stop.

"It's time." Alex said and both of us stepped out.

I opened the door, let my feet hit the ground and stretched my arms up. This is one of the moments I've been waiting for. It took me some time to find what's behind the door but now that the truth is out, it was worth the search.

I walked in and down the hallway with a smile on my face. I couldn't believe it's been six months and I was coming face to face with the person I never met. One of the guards opened the door and there she was in a pack and play looking like my daughter, her sister Arcelia. She turned around and put her little hands up for me to hold her. It was funny because this is my first time meeting her. I guess she knows who her father is. I sat her on my lap and thought about how I found them.

"MJ, what are you doing here? How... did you..." Carlotta asked when she stepped out the shower and noticed me on the bed.

"Is that anyway to greet the man you claimed to love? Or the man you violated and stole sperm from?"

"MJ, you enjoyed it." She said as if she tried to believe it herself. I ran over to the wall she refused to move from.

"Bitch, you drugged me and..." she cut me off.

"I'm sorry. I love you and.-"

"Love would've never allowed you to almost kill me, just to have my kid. Matter of fact, where is the baby?"

"MJ please."

"You know how I feel about people begging once they get caught." As soon as I said that, we heard a baby cry.

"Alex, get the baby and take her to abuela's. The doctor will be there shortly to take a DNA." He nodded and did what I asked. I didn't want to look at her and become attached. What if she weren't mine? Even though she resembled Le Le in the photos, it could still be a coincidence. I heard the front door close and got down to business with Carlotta.

"MJ, please don't take my baby. I swear, I won't bother you or.-" I put my finger to her lips and let it roam down to her neck, the top of her chest and soon after unwrapped the towel for what's to come next. Carlotta was indeed a bad bitch but she fucked up violating me.

"If that's my baby, Morgan will be her mother. There will be no memories of you whatsoever. It will be as if Morgan birthed her."

"How when they are close in age?" They were only a week apart from what she said in all the messages she would send.

"That's right. Well, I'll have it put on paper that they're fraternal twins. Thanks for reminding me. I would hate to have Camila grow up, unsure about things."

"Who is Camila?"

"Oh that's my daughter's name if she's mine."

"But that's not what I named her."

"Ugh, do you really think I care? Plus, since they're going to be considered twins, their name should be similar. Now, lets get to what's about to happen."

"MJ please." She was hysterical crying as she begged for her life when the two guys stepped in.

"Carlotta, I was good to you. I never treated you like shit, you held it down in the bedroom and I gave you what you wanted as far as money, gifts an other shit."

"I didn't want any of it. I only wanted you." I had to laugh. She said that but didn't return a damn thing or showed me any different.

"Carlotta, you know who I am. What, you thought because of the child it would make me feel sorry?" I nodded my head and the two guys made their way to her.

"What the fuck are they doing? Get off me."

"Oh these are some people on my team that are going to do the same thing to you, that you did to me." I stood there laughing and watching her try to fight them off.

"You're going to let them rape me?"

"This isn't rape Carlotta." I made my way over to her as one guy started to take his shirt off.

"It's what you want. Don't worry, you'll enjoy it." Her mouth dropped open. I walked out the room and sat in the living room waiting for them to finish. Call me what you want but the Bible says, do unto others as you want done to you.

Now who am I not to give Carlotta exactly what she gave me? I mean granted, it's a little different but I wouldn't be MJ if I took it easy.

After a while both dudes came out slapping hands with one another without a care in the world. They informed me of how good of a time they both had.

Phew! Phew!

I shot both of them in the head, stepped over their bodies and went in the room. You ask why I did that when they were only doing what I asked. Well, if a man will rape a woman for his boss, he'll rape anyone. I can't have those two running around my streets thinking it's ok.

I opened the bedroom door and Carlotta was laid out. She was beaten so bad her face was unrecognizable. Her body had bruises on it and blood was leaking from down below. I stared at her, pointed my gun at her forehead and emptied my entire clip in her body. I felt no remorse for taking away my daughters mother and no one was going to make me.

Now I'm sitting here in my abuela's house holding my daughter for the first time. I felt a tear fall down my face as I stared. Carlotta made me miss out on a lot of time with her, all because she was being petty.

Camila clapped her hands and sucked on her binky as she stared at me. I removed it and I swear her and Le Le were definitely twins. I picked up my phone and called Morgan. I planned on waiting for her to get here to mention it but I wanted to see where her head was.

"Hey baby." She answered in a sexy voice.

"Hey. You coming home tonight?"

"Yup. Le Le and I are getting ready now. She misses her daddy and I miss him too." I laughed in the phone. Morgan was definitely a nympho.

"Babe, I need you to sit down for a minute."

"Is everything ok?" She instantly went into panic mode.

"Yea. I'm going to face time you but I need you to be ok with what you see."

"Miguel, if you're hurt, I don't want to see it. I'm leaving now and.-"

"Relax baby. I'm fine. Just answer when I call." I went to dial her number back and heard some commotion at my abuela's door. I stood up and walked down the hall to see what was going on.

"WHAT THE FUCK ARE YOU DOING HERE?" My daughter jumped from the bass in my voice. At this moment I was pissed for telling my security not to follow me here. I didn't want anyone around me when I met my daughter for the first time. I heard my phone with the face time ring tone. I must've been taking too long to call Morgan back.

"What I should've done a long time ago." I felt a sharp pain.

"Did you just shoot me with my daughter in my arms?" I looked and my abuela was on the ground.

"Look at it this way. You don't care who you kill so when I take her life, we can call it even." Another shot was fired and all I saw was red.

TO BE CONTINUED...

CPSIA information can be obtained
at www.ICGtesting.com
Printed in the USA
LVOW13s1432150218
566731LV00022B/621/P